THE COMMON HOURS

TINA D. STEPHENS

16.95

ISBN: 978-1-4834-3152-9 (sc)
ISBN: 978-1-4834-3151-2 (e)

Library of Congress Control Number: 2015907759

Because of the dynamic nature of the Internet, any web addresses or links contained in this book may have changed since publication and may no longer be valid. The views expressed in this work are solely those of the author and do not necessarily reflect the views of the publisher, and the publisher hereby disclaims any responsibility for them.

Any people depicted in stock imagery provided by Thinkstock are models, and such images are being used for illustrative purposes only. Certain stock imagery © Thinkstock.

Lulu Publishing Services rev. date: 05/15/2015

To Bonnie
Not just a sister but a friend too.

WITH GRATITUDE

It is with much appreciation, I recognize the following people who helped complete this book: my sister, Bonnie Truax, for her encouragement to keep writing; Christa Coe, for her invaluable knowledge on period food, medicine, and language for the 1800's; Trinity Montero, for his insightful editing and feedback, which pushed the book to be better; Sharon Smith who fixed my grammar and all my extra "that's" that I like to write; Ben Reynolds who took the final edit to make it a polished copy.

I am also grateful to Makenzie McKown who agreed to be the face behind "Mary" and the inspiration for the artwork in the book. Thank you Katherine Schmalz for your talent, which added beauty to the book. Thank you everyone.

CONTENTS

CHAPTER 1

Loss

Williamsport, Pennsylvania, July, 1888.

Sarah sat up, her chest pounding with the vague recollection of her dreams, her skin damp from the muggy air. Dim light from the gas lamp on the street, two stories below, was streaming through her open window. Looking around she slowly evaluated everything in the room. Her robe was still hanging over the end of the iron bed frame; her dress was still draped over the back of the wicker chair in the corner. Nothing was out of place. Her breathing calmed with the confirmation that it was a dream that had woken her up.

Before she could settle under her covers again, shuffling in the hallway drew her attention to the bedroom door. Soft, hurried feet ran past, followed closely by a heavier set of feet. Sarah swung her legs over the edge of the bed. In the dark her toes found their way into her slippers. She crept slowly toward the door hoping the floorboards would not creak. The glass doorknob slipped in her sweaty hand so she grabbed it tighter, gently turning the knob. She could see the tall figure of her father disappearing down the stairway. Sarah snuck out the door. She crept past her parents' bedroom then crossed over to the opposite wall where she could see downstairs.

In the foyer, her mother was sitting with her back against the wall, her head buried in her hands. Her father knelt next to her, close enough to whisper in her ear. "Mary, I love you."

"John—I'm lonely." Her voice lowered at the last word. "I tried to tell you how alone I feel."

Sarah could hear her father's voice shake as he spoke. "Mary, I know I have been working long hours, but—I was doing it to provide for you and Sarah."

"I wish you had been here more."

"So it's my fault?" He sounded defensive.

"That's not what I meant—I'm so confused."

Her father leaned his head against the wall, his gaze toward the ceiling. In the brief silence Sarah could feel her heart pounding in her chest; she was alarmed by what was happening.

Her father spoke again. "What are you expecting from me, Mary?"

Her mother stood, pausing briefly, as if she was making up her mind about something. "I'm leaving." She opened the front door, ran past the hydrangeas and the rope swing, through the iron gate, and into the thick morning fog.

Sarah waited for her father to go after her, but he didn't. She hollered out from the top of the stairway, "No!" Sarah ran down the stairs, brushing past her stoic father as she headed outside. The predawn light was filtering through the fog, the streetlamps casting dim yellow orbs. Bare feet carried her in the direction her mother had gone on the wet slate walkway. It was quiet, except for the pounding of her feet on the stone slabs. *Please don't let her go, God. Please don't let her go.*

No matter how far she ran there was no sight of her mother. A single wagon passing on the other side of the street distracted her attention so much so that Sarah didn't see the slate slab that was lifted higher by a stray tree root. She tripped and fell face-first on the walkway. Tears ran down her cheeks as she slammed her fists onto the ground, one fist after the other. A pair of arms picked her up from the walkway. She fell back into her father's chest, crying.

CHAPTER 2

Change

Bordered by low-lying cornfields and expansive horse pastures, the Susquehanna River flows slowly in the month of July on its path into Williamsport, Pennsylvania. As the river flows closer to the city into the west branch of the Susquehanna River, fields are replaced with sawmills and log ponds. Once an agricultural town, the lumber industry brought people from everywhere, to cash in on the lumber business that made Williamsport the millionaire capital of the country.

Sarah lived on the corner of Fourth and Walnut Streets in the middle of what had been nicknamed "Millionaire Row." The Richardson home was a redbrick Victorian. Shutters and gables were painted teal with accents of terra cotta. Above the front porch railing, which spanned the length of the house, hung four Boston ferns. The gardens in front of the house were overflowing with purple lilacs, yellow carnations, and red chrysanthemums. Blue hydrangea shrubs reached high over the gardens bordering the stairway from the porch to the slate stepping-stone pathway to the front gate. A single rope swing with a wood-plank seat hung from the black walnut tree in the front yard. An ornate black iron fence separated the yard from the slate sidewalk.

This morning Sarah walked to the river to think. She sat down on a grassy bank under the Market Street Bridge and watched the early-morning sun sparkling off the green water. To the north a system of man-made islands and chained logs called the boom funneled the flow of the river into the west branch. The boom was built to collect lumber from the spring log drives. When melting snow made the creeks and rivers flow higher, the woodhicks pushed all the harvested lumber downstream to Williamsport. Once the inventory reached Williamsport, young boys called boom rats would balance across the logs, looking for markings from the sawmills so they could sort them into the lumber mill log ponds. In summer, the waterways were too shallow for the log drives, so the river for now was at peace.

Sarah breathed deeply. Orange tiger lilies bloomed in a thick patch where the steep grassy bank met the bridge. A breeze coming from the river smelled mossy, the damp air already heating up in the early-morning hours. Wet hair was clinging to Sarah's neck, so she reached back to twist the dark brunette locks into a sloppy knot above her neck. It was July 15, 1888, one week before her fourteenth birthday. There was nothing exceptional about it, except change was happening and she was powerless to stop it.

Her mother hadn't returned home since leaving early this morning. The whispers she had overheard between her parents were re-playing themselves in her head. Sarah's parents had never fought before. She couldn't imagine why her father had let her mother go.

The river was her thinking spot, the place where she found peace by listening to the water and watching the wildlife. A sound from the river caught her attention. A boy in a white rowboat midstream was casting a fishing line out into the water. It splashed through the surface with a small ripple that bounced out into three bigger ripples. Further downstream on the banks of the Susquehanna sat the gleaming white building of Revival Bible Church. The sound of the organ and the choir preparing for morning service drifted out over the river like a soothing lullaby, the words indistinguishable.

The church sat horizontal to the river. From her vantage point, Sarah could see the staircase and platform that reached up to the open double doors. A tall rosebush on each side of the stairway bloomed red with flowers. The tall steeple reached above the sycamore trees.

The church's preacher, Reverend Claythorn, had come to Williamsport like a summer storm with his sudden appearance and bold declarations. He stood well over six feet tall, was as broad as two men, and had black hair that curved down over his forehead. Reverend Claythorn's deep voice demanded attention. Mrs. Pratt, who ran the general store on Market Street, said his voice sounded like the voice of God.

Within a year of coming to town his tent meetings became so popular he decided to have a permanent structure built. He named it Revival Bible Church because he believed all the lumbermen needed revival from their greedy ways. The church had six tall windows on each side of the building to represent the twelve disciples. The windows were made tall to draw one's gaze to heaven and not the things of this earth. Reverend Claythorn claimed to have been given strict instructions from God himself to build in the exact spot where it now sat.

A blue heron was standing perfectly still in the shallow waters near the church. When the young fisherman tossed his line into the water again, the heron unfolded his wings and glided to shallow water on the other side. A wagon came over the bridge taking the dirt road toward the church. Sarah knew she had little time left before church began, but she wasn't anxious to leave her place of reverie.

Two more wagons came over the bridge. People were gathering in front of the building. Dark clouds were rising over the ridge of mountains to the west, rumbling occasionally with thunder. She sighed with relief. At least the rain would cool the air down for a little while.

A young, blond-haired girl in a long white dress was running toward her from the church. It was her cousin Katherine whom she called "Kassie." Kassie was not only her cousin, but also her best friend. Sarah stood up, brushed grass off the back of her dress, and prepared herself for the scolding she would get from Kassie for being late to service.

Kassie liked to follow the rules more closely than she did. She smiled when Kassie stopped, out of breath, to put her hands on her knees and holler out to her, "Sarah—get over here! Church has already begun."

Kassie took another deep breath then stood up with her hands on her hips, giving Sarah a scolding look. Sarah plucked a small purple flower from a nearby bush and stuck it in her hair before running to her cousin.

"Sarah, you're going to get me in trouble one of these days." Kassie took another big breath, "The choir is singing the first song!"

Kassie ran toward the stairs followed by Sarah, whose hair tumbled out of the knot of hair she had tied, into long messy strands. As soon as they entered the double red doors, the stale air from inside gushed out at them. The church was full. Everyone was standing and singing. The music had a lazy drawl. It was too hot to sing any other way.

"Shall we gather at the river—"

Women were cooling themselves with paper fans. The choir was singing along with the organ. Mr. Morgan was leading the congregation by waving his hands to the time of the music. As a young man in the army, Mr. Morgan had led the marching band. It was comical to watch him lead the congregation with the same gusto of an army bandleader. His arms waved back and forth in jerky movements, which bounced the thin hair on the top of his balding head.

"The beautiful, the beautiful river;
Gather with the saints at the river—"

Another distant rumble of thunder was barely audible above the sound of the organ. The long rectangular building was lined with polished wood floors and two rows of long pews. The floor was already dusty from the number of shoes that had walked on it this morning. Kassie and Sarah stepped quietly down the aisle toward the front pew where their families always sat. Both Uncle Jacob and her father were deacons in the church, so they made their families sit up front. Sarah had always thought it would be more interesting to sit in the back where she could watch everyone. Dusty Palmer, a first-grader from school, stuck his tongue out at Sarah as she walked by. She squinted down at him with what she called her "evil eye" look. He quickly looked away, and she smirked to herself.

The congregation was finishing the last chorus when they reached the front pew. Kassie went to the right to sit with her brother, Elijah, and mother, Aunt Katherine. Sarah stepped left to where her mother usually sat next to Mrs. Pratt and her grandson, Jude.

Sarah's father was up front on the platform in a pew that sat before the choir box, next to the other deacons and Reverend Claythorn. She sat next to Jude, not surprised at the absence of her mother. Jude was five and adored Sarah. He was wearing grey knickers with a white shirt and a black ribbon tied at his throat. His blond little head and blue eyes looked over at Sarah who smiled in return.

Thunder clapped loudly overhead, causing everyone to jump. Jude grabbed Sarah's arm briefly. Mrs. Pratt let out a little gasp. Reverend Claythorn walked to the podium on the raised platform. Sarah was amazed he still wore his suit coat in the intense heat. Reverend Claythorn was always a picture of perfect decorum. He placed his large black Bible on the podium and looked out over the congregation. Sarah noticed his hands, which gripped the flat surface of the podium, were trembling, but his face was composed. Everyone was silent, waiting in anticipation for the fiery exposition they would hear today. Reverend Claythorn briefly looked back at his deacons then over the congregation again. He cleared his throat. It was so quiet Sarah could hear the whir of the paper fan Mrs. Pratt was vigorously waving to cool herself. A fly buzzed against a windowpane at the end of their pew. Sweat rolled down her neck. Reverend Claythorn pulled a hanky out of his vest to wipe his forehead dry.

"Brothers and sisters—on this day I am reflecting over the first moments I came to Williamsport, a city threatened with the vengeance of God by its carnal inhabitants; a city of men void of counsel and filled with greed. Nothing could keep them from hell but God."

Reverend Claythorn's deep voice hushed even the children. He stood tall, oblivious to the droplets of sweat rolling down his temples.

"My observation is this—there are still many on the brink of a pit with no discernment of their ways. This building stands as a beacon to guide them away from the brink of destruction. Do not imagine or pretend this will not come under all manner of difficulty. You must press forward in the power of God!

Henceforth—" He cleared his throat then looked back at the deacons again. The deacons remained stoic in return. He faced the congregation again. Mrs. Pratt's fan paused in motion. "I am beckoned to a new town on the brink of its own destruction, a people that has not even a breath of air between them and hell. It is therefore with great urgency I leave this place. I pray that you will not suffer greatly, but that you will find encouragement. May God's blessing be with you."

All the deacons stood up. With his head slightly down, Reverend Claythorn placed his Bible under his arm, walked off the platform, down the aisle, and out the back door. The deacons followed him. Everyone was so stunned by what had happened, it wasn't until he was out the door that the crying and the murmuring began.

Sarah looked around at the confusion taking over the congregation. Choir members were crying and hugging each other. Women were running over to other women, hugging and whispering. The men spoke quietly in subdued groups. Small children were clinging to their mothers' dresses, confused by the disorder. Sarah looked in Kassie's direction, but her cousin was gone. Women behind her were whispering loudly,

"Can you believe it?"

"It's a scandal like we've never seen before—"

"Caught yesterday—at the Reverend's home no less."

"Did she think what this would do to her family?"

"John forced him to leave, or else."

Sarah turned around at the mention of her father's name. The women were startled to see Sarah near enough to hear them. They moved toward the aisle talking in more hushed tones. Sarah's eyes were brimming with tears. Mrs. Pratt placed a hand on her shoulder giving her a sympathetic look.

Thunder clapped overhead again, louder than the chaos inside. Sarah ran down the aisle to find where her father had gone. He would know what was happening. When she reached the doors, a gust of wind blew dust in her eyes briefly blinding her. She leaned against the stair railing to look in the direction of the deacons who were standing together under the trees by the wagons, near the dirt road.

When she spotted her father standing on the far side of their wagon, she ran to him. "Father, what's going on? Where's mother?"

Her father reached an arm around her shoulders but his gaze remained fixed on the road. She looked toward the road too. Reverend Claythorn's retreating wagon was kicking up dust behind it. Thunder clapped. A large drop of water hit her face, then another and another until the rain came down in a sudden loud gush. The deacons scattered to gather their families. Wagons left in a rush to get home.

One wagon remained. Sarah and her father stood oblivious to the rain, staring at the road. The rain dripped down their skin, soaking their clothing, then continued its course in snaking rivulets across the dirt lot, through the grass yard, down the riverbanks, and into the river.

Mary

CHAPTER 3

Leaving

Mary stood in the alley between Fourth and Walnut Streets, across from her home. In the hours after fleeing the house, she struggled with the idea of leaving her family but finally concluded she would only return to gather a few things while her family was away at church. She was standing under a small window overhang that provided some shelter from the weather. She was shivering in her already rain-soaked clothing and hair. A wagon with a single driver passed slowly on the street then it was quiet. Mary took the opportunity to dart across the street to her yard. Under the hydrangea shrubs was a house key for the front door. Looking again at the street and over at her brother-in-law's home, she assured herself that no one was home from church.

As Mary walked upstairs, she ran her hand along the wide banister, trying to seal in memories of happiness, loneliness, and heartbreak. In the bedroom, she put a satchel on the bed. Needing to travel light, she took only what was necessary out of the dresser drawers. The wardrobe in the corner was slightly open. She pulled the sleeve of a brown jacket out, smelling deeply of her John, glancing briefly at the fancy dresses hanging next to his suits.

In the top drawer of her bureau, she reached along the right side where her dress gloves were stacked. A small envelope was hidden, flat against the wood bottom. She carefully placed the envelope in the front pocket of her bag, along with some rag money she had saved.

Mary reached for her bag then remembered one last thing. Under her side of the bed was a package for Sarah's birthday next week. She took it, along with her bag, across the hall to Sarah's room. Sarah had left her window open letting the breeze flow in. Dress shoes stood on the floor next to her daughter's bed. Mary smiled, knowing that Sarah got away with wearing her casual shoes to church.

"That girl—probably walked along the river before church!"

Mary held the brown package with blue ribbon close to her chin as she looked around Sarah's room. She ran her hand along the cross patchwork calico quilt she made for her daughter. Last fall the quilt was in the parlor downstairs stretched out over the quilting frame. For hours Sarah would sit next to her learning the intricate stitches that bound the quilt together.

One afternoon Sarah asked if she could draw while her mother sewed.

"What are you drawing Sarah?"

"You, Mother. I don't want to forget how you look in the light coming through the window, as you work on my quilt."

Mary pulled a thread up through the quilt. "You see beauty in so many things Sarah. I hope you never lose that ability." She remembered telling her daughter, "I am making this quilt so you will always have something close to remind you of how much I love you."

Mary sat down on her daughter's bed, overtaken by emotion. She could feel the tears sliding down her cheeks as she clutched the brown package close to her. Tears soaked a corner of the wrapping. She ran her hand over the stitches of the quilt, wondering if her daughter would remember.

Thunder overhead startled her back to reality. Outside a wagon came close then turned into the drive between their home and her brother in-law Jacob's home. Panicked, she realized it was Jacob and his family returning home from church. She had little time to escape unseen while he pulled the wagon into the barn behind the house. She left the gift on Sarah's bed then ran downstairs.

There would be enough time, hopefully, to get away before any of the family would be near a front window to see her. Rain was coming down hard. She locked the front door glancing toward Jacob's place. No curtains were moving, which meant no one was looking outside. She crossed the street without watching for oncoming wagons. Before reaching the walkway on the other side, she slipped on a patch of mud and fell down on her backside. Her tailbone stung but she picked herself up and ran into the alley, breathing hard. One more look at her brother-in-law's place confirmed the curtains were still undisturbed.

Careful to not expose the paper to rain, she pulled out the envelope from the front pocket of her bag. She read an address written on the paper inside:

Caroline Oakley
31 Mill Street
Trout Run, Pennsylvania

In spite of her exhaustion, Mary could not sleep on the stagecoach ride that followed the Lycoming Creek north to the town of Trout Run. Two well-dressed gentlemen sat across from her on the cushioned seat. They were, gratefully, asleep. Mary felt less nervous about being discovered in the closed coach, but still couldn't relax into the seat. The storm had quieted. Fog was rising up into the night air.

The stagecoach stopped briefly at a railroad crossing near the mouth of Lycoming Creek to wait for a train to pass by. The conductor blew his whistle and waved out his window as he passed the stagecoach. She closed her eyes against memories suddenly filling her mind.

Mary was nine years old the last time she had seen her mother, Caroline. Her mother was mopping the floor in the kitchen the last day she was home. Her father was headed out the door to check on a broken railroad switch.

"Ben, can you take her along with you so I can mop the rest of the house?"

He seemed irritated with her for asking. "Hopefully she doesn't get in my way."

Mary remembered how the sun sparkled off the dew on the tall grass of the hayfields near their home, how a robin rose up from the road as they walked by. At the bottom of the knoll was the track in need of repair. A large boulder conveniently sat at the edge of the pathway near the tracks on which she rested while her father worked on the switch.

Two tracks converged here, and a train was due soon. The lever to switch the train to the correct track was stuck. Her father was swearing under his breath as he worked on the switch. With a grunt of strength he pulled back on the lever. It snapped toward him unexpectedly, causing his foot to slip down into the crossing tracks as the action of the lever moved the tracks together. His shoe was trapped. Mary's head jerked up at the sound of a train whistle. He tugged on his leg to pull it out of the shoe. It didn't budge. The laces were tied high up on his work boots. He anxiously worked at loosening the knots. Standing near the rock, Mary looked toward the train, now visible, then at her father whose hands were moving fast. The train neared, he pulled on his shoe again. Chest heaving with panic she ran up the hill, away from the train and her father and away from what she knew was about to happen. Before the train hit him, the whistle blew loudly over the sound of her father crying out. Mary only stopped for a moment hearing the train whistle blow and the high screech of brakes on the metal rails of the track. Mary ran away.

Two days after the accident, a couple headed toward Williamsport, found her walking along a road, hungry and delirious. They took her to their home. She told them her family was killed in a house fire, and her name was "Mary." No one since that time knew about her past. Over the years she blocked it from her memory.

Mary's thoughts were interrupted when the stagecoach came to an abrupt stop at the hotel in Trout Run. The two gentlemen across from her were already gathering their things from below the seat. They motioned for her to exit ahead of them. She grabbed her bag, which she had placed on the seat next to her. The driver opened the door to help her down.

Standing on the hotel steps looking out into the thick fog, she wondered how she would find her way to the address on the paper.

One of the gentlemen must have noticed her lost look. "Is anyone coming to meet you?"

Mary reached into her bag for the paper she had placed there, "Do you know where Thirty One Mill Street is?"

She looked up in time to see him smile. She assumed he knew where it was.

"It's a little walk from here, especially in the fog. I will ask the driver to take you to Mill Street. Once he drops you off, you will see a large smoke stack from the paper mill. This address is—"

He paused, looking at the number again.

"—I am pretty sure this is behind the paper mill near the creek." He smiled again. "If you end up in the water, you will know you have gone too far, and you never know what can happen in this kind of fog." He laughed at his own joke.

"Thank you." Mary was having second thoughts about her decision to visit her mother.

The gentleman talked to the driver who agreed to make the stop on his way north. When she reached Mill Street, she looked up at the high smoke stack of the paper mill whose top disappeared into the fog. Her mother's home was three houses behind the mill.

Mary stepped onto the front porch of the house. A single lantern in the front window glowed warmly through lace curtains pulled shut. She stood in front of the door, not ready to knock. The sound of the creek was close. Bullfrogs called loudly one to another in raspy tones.

Mary wondered if her mother would know who she was. She knocked softly with the hope no one would answer. Absentmindedly, she turned her right shoe slightly sideways, in order to walk away. Leaving was how she always dealt with her problems. The door opened, light filtering out over a short, fragile figure.

The voice was soft. "Who is it?" The woman stepped slightly back into the light, high cheekbones shadowed, grey hair swept up into a bun.

Mary rushed forward with sudden emotion, hugging the woman tight to herself.

The woman was startled, "Leia?"

CHAPTER 4

Sleepless

Sarah lay on her bed in her second-story bedroom overlooking the front yard. The lance-shaped leaves of the black walnut tree in the front yard were casting shadows on the tongue and groove ceiling. Brown and pink calico curtains hung straight in the damp air. She didn't recall walking up the stairs to her bedroom or her father sitting in the wing back chair in the parlor room downstairs after they arrived home from church. The dark house was eerily quiet. The clip-clop of horses' hooves from passing wagons echoed out over the stillness.

In her hands she held the brown paper package left on her bed. She fingered the tag on which her name was scrawled. Her mother must have been here while they were at church. There was no note on the gift.

She replayed the speech Reverend Claythorn gave this morning, the look on the faces of the church people, the continued absence of her mother, and the whispers from the women who had been sitting near her.

She remembered the image of her mother disappearing out the front door into the early morning fog. She thought about Reverend Claythorn's wagon leaving the church. A cricket started calling from somewhere in the yard; another one near the river answered it.

She wanted to believe that Reverend Claythorn's leaving had nothing to do with her mother's leaving. When the clock tower at Trinity Episcopal Church gonged eleven times, she realized sleep would not come easily.

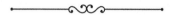

A thunderstorm awoke Sarah in the early hours of morning. The events of yesterday seemed like distant dreams but the exhaustion and the emptiness she felt inside were evidence of their reality. She barely had the will to move from her bed. Sarah rolled on her side to watch the curtains breathe slowly back and forth in the breeze. Droplets of rain on the windowpanes reflected the morning light.

Without the desire to get up, she fell asleep again. A gentle knock on her door an hour later startled her out of a dream about her mother. Another knock this time was followed by a whisper: "Sarah, it's Kassie."

Sarah remained silent.

"Are you awake?"

The door slowly creaked open. Even though Sarah's back was to the door she could envision Kassie looking cautiously at her bed. Sarah opened her eyes but didn't move. Stepping around the bed, Kassie sat on the edge of the mattress and placed a hand on Sarah's shoulder.

Kassie didn't say anything. Sarah moved her head so she could look directly at Kassie. "Are you here to get me out of bed?"

Kassie looked at her cousin. "The packer boats are running today. I thought I might persuade you to go with me to watch them take off."

The bed bounced as Kassie turned to grab a basket she had with her. She lifted a cream linen cloth to remove one of her homemade specialty muffins always bigger than anyone else's homemade muffins. "Mother let me make the muffins this morning. I always fill the pans too full."

Sarah could envision Aunt Katherine scolding Kassie. She smiled. The muffin smelled wonderful, and hunger was speaking louder than her tiredness.

Kassie was holding a muffin close to Sarah, "You will feel better with something in your stomach."

Sarah took it. Kassie stood up then walked to the door with the basket hooked on her arm, "I'll leave the rest of the muffins on the kitchen table, and then I'll be on the front porch. Don't keep me waiting long."

Sarah took a big bite from the muffin before sitting up in bed to stretch her arms up above her head. Her cousin was right; she needed a diversion to take away the constant replaying of events in her head. Sarah quickly dressed. On her way outside she stopped at the base of the stairs to look into the parlor. Her father was sitting in a chair in the far corner, still dressed in his Sunday suit. "Father, Kassie invited me to go with her to watch the packer boats."

He raised his head to look at her. His eyes were red from lack of sleep. Sarah had never seen her father like this. "Kassie made muffins for us. They are on the kitchen table." She paused, not sure if she should go or if she should stay.

He looked out of the parlor window toward his brother's place. "Go with Kassie."

Kassie and Sarah ran down the sidewalk toward the Exchange Hotel where the packer boats would start their journey to the town of Jersey Shore.

Kassie was clothed in a white dress bordered at the bottom with three rows of lace trim. Blue ribbons held a half-ponytail of blonde hair. Sarah was in her brown calico blouse with short puffy sleeves and a long brown skirt. She wore her ankle-high river shoes. Kassie always scolded Sarah about wearing boy shoes. Sarah liked how practical they were when she was running along the river or in the forest. She knew no one could see what kind of shoes were under her long skirt. What mattered most was she could run.

They neared the noise of Market Street named for all of the curbside markets. Trolleys ran constantly back and forth on the dirt road that led away from the river. Women with umbrellas and large hats roamed the streets. A number of men in suits walked the streets going about their business; others were dressed casually for their work at the lumber mills.

Sarah ran alongside Kassie, dodging market stands and wagons. It was good to feel the movement of her feet one in front of the other. She could run. She could breathe. Kassie was with her. She was living in spite of everything going on in her life.

A crew of men, at The Exchange Hotel, were loading the packer boats and tethering ropes to the horses that would pull the boats. The packer boats were wide platforms on which sat a house box with wooden benches affixed to the flat roof. Women in fancy dresses and umbrellas were already docking. When everything and everyone were finally on board, the horses began to pull. Following the journey of the boat, Kassie and Sarah ran along the riverbank on a narrow footpath. They were jumping over rocks and swampy puddles, sometimes with their arms out to their sides, laughing and smiling. The cloudless sky was sapphire. When the boat reached a wide bend in the river, the girls stopped breathless to drop down in a meadow tall with grass and yellow dandelions.

Kassie spoke in a whisper, not sure if she should ask the question on her mind, "Do you want to talk about it?"

Sarah was quick to respond. "No."

A grasshopper jumped onto Sarah's blouse. She looked down at its bulging eyes, before flicking it on its way. "Not really—but I wish I knew what was going on." Sarah sat up to face Kassie, sitting with her legs crossed underneath her.

Kassie sat up too, playing with blades of grass between her fingers. "I'm sorry, Sarah."

They were both quiet for a couple of minutes, chewing on blades of grass and snapping dandelion tops from their base.

If she was going to talk to anyone, Kassie was the one who knew her best. "I can't make sense of everything that happened yesterday."

Kassie spoke hesitantly, "I can tell you what I overheard on Saturday."

Sarah looked up, eager for any information she could get.

Kassie could see her cousin's eagerness so she continued speaking. "Late in the afternoon mother was working in the garden at the back of the house when Aunt Mary came into the yard. She was very upset. She kept telling Mother she made a terrible mistake and ruined her family's reputation. I overheard Aunt Mary asking for help to run away. Mother wouldn't hear of her running away, and told her she would help in any other way she could. She put an arm around Aunt Mary telling her everything would be okay, but Aunt Mary could not be consoled. 'You don't know what I have done!'" Kassie looked at Sarah whose brow was furrowed in worry.

It took awhile before Sarah spoke. "I hardly know what to feel, Kassie. This is so sudden and unbelievable!" Sarah knew by Kassie's expression there was more to tell. "What else do you know?"

"Sarah, this is really hard for me to tell you. That evening, after what happened in the garden, father came home upset. He took mother into the parlor to talk. I know that I shouldn't have—but I snuck down the stairs to listen by the door. He told mother Uncle John had stopped by Reverend Claythorn's place earlier and found Reverend Claythorn and Aunt Mary—" She paused. "—Reverend Claythorn was kissing Aunt Mary. When she saw Uncle John leaving the front porch she ran outside to him. Uncle John left without speaking to her. Later he returned to the parsonage demanding Reverend Claythorn to resign and to leave town immediately, or else."

Before the end of the story, tears were running down Sarah's face. Kassie reached over to wrap her arms around Sarah. They cried together. Sarah wondered if her mother still loved her father. Did her mother still love her? When they could no longer cry, they rested in the grass with their arms folded under the back of their heads. They watched the puffy clouds overhead trying to forget what was going on with their families. An hour later, hunger reminded them to go home.

John woke up in the white Victorian armchair in the parlor. He sat up stretching out his stiff back then leaned forward to put his head in his hands. Looking down at his wool trousers, he realized he hadn't changed since church yesterday. The last two days rushed through his mind. He exhaled in disbelief and exhaustion.

He pulled his pocket watch out of his vest. It was already 8:00 a.m. In spite of everything that had taken place he needed to go into the office today.

Remembering what Sarah had said about the muffins on the kitchen table, he headed in that direction. If Mary were here she would have already filled the kitchen with the aroma of baking. Morning light, from the window over the sink, was subtly lighting the kitchen. He opened the icebox; it felt warm inside. He seemed to recollect Mary had ice delivered on occasion, yet another thing he would have to figure out how to do.

Carefully, he pulled the water pan out from under the icebox to empty it into the sink. He found the muffins in a basket on the table. Muffin in hand, he climbed the stairs to his room, their room, and when he reached the bedroom door a sense of dread filled him. He turned the doorknob and paused. Mary was gone. His lifelong friend was gone.

He took a deep breath, opened the door, and readied himself for the day, pushing down the feelings that wanted to surface. He would be in the office all day so he put on another brown suit.

The walk to the office took him down Maynard Street, across two railroad tracks, and over the log ponds used for sorting lumber. The office was a square wood building near the ponds, and a sign over the porch read Richardson Brothers Lumberyard. John and his brother Jacob had started the Lumberyard, eighteen years ago, before either of them had married. Jacob was good at keeping the books; John enjoyed working with the woodhicks in the lumberyard. He was also good at keeping the peace between the sometimes-unruly men. He knew his brother Jacob would already be at the office.

When he opened the door and hung his suit jacket on the peg behind the door, he thought about walking out again. He didn't want to face the awkwardness of his situation, but he couldn't ignore his brother who had already seen him walk in.

"John."

John turned around.

Jacob hugged him. "John. I would have understood if you had chosen to not come in today."

John stepped back walking over to his desk. "I didn't know what else to do."

Jacob spoke his idea. "Did you have breakfast yet?"

John smiled. "Kassie brought muffins over this morning before her and Sarah headed outside."

"A muffin is hardly a breakfast. Let's go to the hotel restaurant by the bridge for hot breakfast and rhubarb pie."

John paused looking at the pile of legal documents on his desk. He picked up the stack of papers for his brother to see. "I need to look at these railroad documents today."

Jacob looked at the documents with disinterest. "It'll make no difference if we wait until tomorrow to read the documents. What the railroad executives say in those papers may change soon, as I have heard rumors that the government is going to intervene on the side of the lumber mills."

Jacob waited by the door for his brother.

John could see that he had no choice in the matter. "You have always put food in front of duty, Jacob."

They walked two blocks and crossed the railroad tracks to arrive at the restaurant. John was grateful to be walking in the warm morning air instead of sitting in the stale office, and breakfast did sound good too.

His brother ordered steak and eggs with toast. John ordered his favorite, country-fried steak with biscuits and gravy. The aroma from it made John realize how little he had eaten in the last two days. They ate in silence watching the woodhicks walk by on the slate sidewalks. The lumber industry had created a large workforce in Williamsport.

Jacob took a swig of coffee then set his mug down heavily.

"John, I don't really want to talk about this, but I wanted to give you a warning."

"A warning?"

"The deacons met yesterday afternoon then stopped by my place last night."

Looking out the window, John picked up his coffee mug but didn't take a drink. He knew what they wanted.

"They want me to step down as deacon because of what happened?"

"Yes. They are visiting you tonight, to deliver the message. Your old friend, Wilson Porter, looked quite pleased to be the one delivering the message." Jacob paused to take a drink of coffee.

John had always been annoyed Wilson Porter had been selected as head deacon. When they were all in school, Wilson had a crush on Mary. He never forgave John for "taking" her away from him.

Jacob interrupted his thoughts. "I told the deacons I wouldn't go with them on the visit. I also put my resignation in as deacon."

John was upset at this news too, "Don't leave because of me, Jacob."

Jacob was quiet. He forked a potato wedge, dipping it in egg yolk that had puddled on his plate. "John, I'm not sure why I became a deacon in the first place. I never went to church before Reverend Claythorn walked into town with his bold messages. I don't know if I believed in God or if I believed in Reverend Claythorn."

"What now, Jacob? Although nothing specific was said, I know everyone is whispering about what really happened. Everyone knows our families. We own one of the biggest sawmills in town. I live on millionaire row!"

Jacob reached into his vest pocket for something. "This might be an answer to your problem. I received a letter from Virginia. She would love to have either of us, along with our family, come north to Slate Run for a little while. She wrote that the Pennsylvania Joint Land and Lumber Company in Slate Run is harvesting trees in the Pine Creek Gorge to float down to Williamsport next May in the spring drive. The James B. Weed and Company has a sawmill in Slate Run that is cutting its own boards and sending them down on the train and harvesting hemlock bark for the tanneries. The Pennsylvania Joint Land and Lumber people are looking for someone to oversee their production to make sure there are no clashes between the two crews. She knows either of us has the experience they are looking for. The company provides a cabin and a barn at the edge of town, for housing while on the job."

John swallowed a piece of steak before it was chewed enough. It went down his throat in a large lump, which he quickly washed down with a gulp of coffee. He put his mug back down on the red-checkered tablecloth.

"How will uprooting Sarah and myself help anything?"

"It might be good for you and Sarah to get away from the gossip for a while. Virginia will be a good influence for Sarah, who has just lost her mother. You can come back in a year or so when people have moved on to another scandal."

"What happens if Mary never returns? People will always be speculating and talking."

The waitress returned to their table and asked if they needed anything else. When she left, Jacob spoke up again. "She left once before and came back."

John wished he hadn't mentioned it. "That was different. Her mother had passed away. She was pregnant with Sarah—."

"John, think about it. I'm giving this letter to you. Go home. I will take care of the legal papers on your desk."

They left the restaurant and John headed over the tracks toward home.

Sarah was gone all day, presumably next door at his brother's house. John was thankful that Sarah had Kassie in her life. Except for a brief job with the railroad when he was younger, he always lived near his brother. When his brother married it was natural for him to build a home next door to John. Moving away was the last thing he would have thought to do.

Sarah arrived home at sunset. She went quietly upstairs to her room. John was in the parlor. He wondered if he should see how she was doing. A knock at the front door interrupted his thought.

When he opened the door Wilson Porter was standing on the front porch with two other deacons from the church. Wilson was looking at John through his spectacles with a smug look on his face. John felt irritated that Wilson was delivering the news, but he remained outwardly polite.

Still on the front porch, Wilson broke the silence, "John, we would like to talk with you for a few minutes."

John opened the door wide and gestured with his hand for them to come inside.

"Sure, Mr. Porter—gentlemen—come right in. Make yourselves at home in the parlor."

They were quiet as they entered the parlor. The two deacons with Wilson were clearly uncomfortable with the situation. They were fidgety in their seats.

John wasn't sure what to say. "I apologize that I am unable to offer you gentlemen ice water. The ice truck left before I arrived home from work today. Would anyone like some coffee?" He hoped the answer would be no because he wasn't sure he could figure out how to brew coffee.

Wilson was sitting at the edge of his seat seemingly anxious to begin. "No, thank you, John—we are fine."

John sat down in a wing-back chair. He crossed his legs then uncrossed them, putting his hands on his lap. Sweat was building on his forehead, which he unconsciously wiped with the back of his hand.

Wilson began, "John, in light of recent events you probably realize we have to ask for your resignation as deacon."

While Wilson looked directly at John, the other deacons kept their eyes on the floor. The sun had set the light slowly evaporating from the parlor. John looked at a small round table in the corner. There was a picture of Mary and him. Her light brown hair was swooped up into a large bun on top of her head. They looked younger and happier in the picture. It was from their engagement seventeen years ago.

Wilson cleared his throat. "John, do you have anything to say?"

John stood up. He felt suddenly alone. His family was broken and theirs were not. "I will comply with your request. It has been a long weekend, and I wish to retire early."

All three men stood, the other two deacons looked relieved at the signal to go.

John gave the last word as they walked out the door. "Give my greetings to your families."

John stood in the middle of the foyer staring at the closed door. He reached up to massage his pounding temples. On the foyer table rested the Bible he had given to Mary after they were engaged. He opened the front cover to read his writing:

Presented to: *Mary Elizabeth Dalton*
From: *John Michael Richardson*
On: *Their engagement to be married, February 14, 1871*

He remembered the day she had consented to marry him and how happy they were as they told their families. John knew they would always be together. He wondered now how things had changed so drastically in seventeen years. Then he remembered the sight of his wife in Reverend Claythorn's arms. A rush of anger came over him. He clenched the Bible in his hands. The image of Mary being kissed by another man wouldn't leave his mind. He threw the Bible across the foyer. It slammed against the wall near the opening to the parlor and slid down, landing on the floor face down open, the pages curved haphazardly in a pile.

A movement from the upstairs hall caught his attention. Sarah was leaving her place from the top step to run back to her room. Her bedroom door slammed. He sat on the bottom stair exhausted. He took the folded letter from his sister out of his pocket. He wondered if leaving town was something he needed to consider.

Sarah heard the deacons leaving the house. She left her room to speak to her father when she witnessed him throwing the Bible against the wall. She ran back to her room frightened by his actions.

Sarah threw herself on her bed and cried herself to sleep. In her dreams she saw Reverend Claythorn's wagon leaving in the rain. She saw her father standing next to her, staring after the retreating wagon. A woman was sitting on the buckboard next to Reverend Claythorn. The woman turned around to blow a kiss in Sarah's direction. When the woman smiled Sarah realized she was looking at her mother.

CHAPTER 5

A Way Out

John's sister-in-law, Katherine, came for a visit the day before Sarah's birthday. John was in the kitchen looking in the icebox when she startled him. "The ice truck comes later today. I will have him deliver some ice for you when he stops at our place."

He stood up quickly, almost hitting his head on an open cupboard door. "Thank you." He closed the icebox door. "I wasn't sure how that worked."

"He will give you a bill that can be paid when he comes again next week." Katherine put a basket on the table. "I brought some fried chicken and biscuits for your dinner. You are always welcome to join us for dinner if you want company."

John walked over to the stove. He had managed to make coffee. "Do you want some coffee?"

"Sure." She sat down at the table. "I wanted to talk to you about something anyway."

He put a mug down in front of her. The liquid looked really dark. "I'd offer you cream—" He looked at the icebox.

"Don't worry about it. I'm sure it will be fine." The look on her face as she glanced at the mug said differently.

"John, tomorrow is July 22."

He sat down. "And?"

"It's your daughter's fourteenth birthday."

John felt tired beyond his years. "Mary always took care of those things."

Katherine didn't seem surprised. "I thought so. Bring Sarah over tomorrow and we will surprise her with a birthday party."

Reaching across the table John closed his hand over hers. "Katherine, I can't thank you enough."

She patted his hands before standing up to leave. "I need you to pick up some colorful streamers from the general store so we can decorate. Her favorite color is blue. While you are at the store, you can also pick out a gift. Mrs. Pratt will help you." Katherine pushed open the back door then paused. "Leave the streamers on your kitchen step. I will send Elijah over to get them this evening."

John followed her to the garden in the backyard. "Katherine—do you think Mary will come back this time?"

Katherine brushed her fingers against the petals of a pink rose at the top of a well-trimmed bush, the product of Mary's meticulous work. "I hope so, John."

Kassie and Sarah had been given pennies for the general store. They were standing in front of a row of six candy jars of horehounds, black licorice, peppermint sticks, taffy, rock candy, and lemon sticks, trying to make up their minds what they wanted. Mrs. Pratt was in the supply room, instructing Mr. Pratt to bring out a 10-pound flour bag for a waiting customer.

The bell on the front door jingled, alerting all another customer was entering. Both girls looked up at the same time to see Wayne Wright, a boy their age, enter. Wayne was a spoiled child who used his boredom to tease the other kids at school. Sarah couldn't stand him, so she turned quickly to the candy again, wondering when Mrs. Pratt would return.

Wayne appeared delighted to see Sarah. He walked right up to the counter and folded his arms on the ledge in front of the candy jars. His blond hair was falling down over his eyes, his freckled nose adding to the mischievous look he was giving through his blue eyes. "Everyone in town is talking about what happened in church on Sunday."

The bell on the door jingled again, but they didn't notice.

Sarah hated him for mentioning Sunday. She was quick to anger. "If you say another word—I'll punch you in the face, Wayne."

"No you won't." He stopped when he heard someone near him clear his throat. He looked up to see Sarah's father standing near them. Wayne ran outside.

Sarah was still red in the face. If Wayne had stayed, she was sure she would have punched him. She didn't say anything to her father who appeared troubled at having witnessed the scene. When Mrs. Pratt returned, Sarah and Kassie decided on yellow candy sticks then quickly left the store.

Sarah was taken by complete surprise at the party her Aunt Katherine and the rest of the family held for her. Kassie gave her a tablet of drawing paper. Her father gave her long dress gloves, her first pair.

"Because you are a young lady now."

He gave her another package containing a pair of high leather boots with a thick traction heel for hiking. He smiled when she looked at him with surprise and delight.

"Because I know you would rather be walking along the river or in the woods than going to a fancy gathering."

She smiled back at him. He knew her so well. "Thank you, Father."

Before she crawled into bed for the night, she remembered the gift her mother left her. Sarah had been saving it for this day. The blue satin ribbons came loose easily to release the folded wrapping. Inside was a set of drawing pencils, paper, and a leather portfolio. Inside the portfolio, was a note:

> *For my daughter,*
> *This is so you can carry your work to the woods and draw*
> *the things you love. You see beauty where others cannot.*
> *Show the world what you see. I will always love you.*
> *Mother*

Sarah knew the letter had been written long before the things that happened on Sunday. A week ago the words would have had different meaning. She wanted to believe her mother loved her, but she left without saying goodbye. Sarah looked at the note again.

> *—I will always love you.*
> *Mother*

In August, one of the deacons started holding services again at church. Two of the deacons shared the responsibility of speaking. The church that used to be standing room only, now had sparsely filled pews. Sarah only knew of this from Kassie telling her. After her father was asked to step down as a deacon, they stopped going to church.

Sarah reached toward her bed stand for her mother's Bible. After her father threw it against the wall the evening the deacons came over, she snuck downstairs in the night to pick it up from the floor. She wanted something of her mother's to remember her by. She read her father's writing, in the front of the Bible, from when they were engaged. She wished things were the way they used to be. Sarah closed the Bible and put it back on the table. She wondered how life would be if her mother never came back.

It was an overcast, cool day when her father came home with the announcement.

"Aunt Virginia wrote us a letter."

Sarah hadn't seen her Aunt Virginia in years but loved reading her descriptive letters of life in the wilderness north of the city. "Is everything all right?"

"They are doing well running the hotel in Slate Run. She wrote to tell me the Pennsylvania Joint Land and Lumber Company is looking for an overseer."

Sarah's brow creased. She put her spoon down in her soup bowl. "Are you seriously thinking about taking the job?"

He seemed to choose his words carefully. "It would be a good opportunity to be near my sister for a while. You could spend time with Aunt Virginia and your cousins. Would it be so bad to be in Slate Run for about a year?"

Sarah couldn't finish her soup. The idea of leaving Kassie behind was incomprehensible. "Would Uncle John and Aunt Katherine come too?"

His answer was quick. "They would not be going."

Sarah was filled with panic. "How soon would we leave if you decide to go?"

Her father cleared his throat. "I've already decided to take the job. We are leaving in two weeks."

Kassie noticed her cousin was quieter than usual. She brought it up two days later when they were raking leaves in the backyard. "You're quiet Sarah. What are you thinking about?"

Sarah didn't even look at Kassie. "Father is taking a job up north where Aunt Virginia and Uncle Harold live."

"What? When?"

Sarah still held her rake, leaning on it slightly. "We leave in two weeks."

Kassie threw her rake down and started pacing the garden. "No! Sarah you can't leave."

"Kassie what can I do? I can't change father's mind. Uncle Jacob told him it was a good idea."

Over the next few days they couldn't stop talking about the move. Kassie knocked on the kitchen door early Friday morning, when Sarah was boiling oatmeal for her father.

Kassie had a copy of the *Williamsport Sun-Gazette* in her hand. "This will change Uncle John's mind."

Sarah looked at the paper confused.

Kassie's finger punched the paper above an article. "Look at the headline in the lower right corner."

Sarah gasped and smiled. "Brilliant!"

Sarah read the headline out loud:

HUMAN BONES FOUND IN SLATE RUN— MAN KILLED BY PANTHER.

"This is perfect, Kassie! I'll put it next to his breakfast this morning!"

Kassie was quick to add, "Be sure to place it just right, with his coffee sitting next to the headline."

"Good idea!"

Kassie assured Sarah of her plan, "Your father won't move away when he sees how dangerous Slate Run is." They both jumped up and down quietly before Kassie left.

When her father came down for breakfast, Sarah kept busy in the kitchen so she could see his reaction. She watched him absentmindedly sip his coffee without a glance at the paper. He barely picked at his oatmeal before grabbing his jacket to leave.

"See you later, Sarah." He bent down to give her a goodbye kiss on the forehead without a single word about the article. She tried to bring it to his attention again by leaving the paper in the parlor where he usually sat in the evening to read. When he finally did notice the article, his only reaction was that he was glad he was good with a gun. Sarah started to pack her things that evening.

Moving day was a week away. Her father explained to her they would take only necessary belongings on the packer boat upriver. In Jersey Shore they would purchase a horse, wagon, and additional supplies for the journey north.

Every extra hour she had was spent with Kassie. They passed the remaining days walking by the river or sitting in the swing on Aunt Katherine's front porch. One afternoon they sat on the porch swing sipping tea. The oak tree in the front yard cast shade over the gardens and the porch. Horse-drawn buggies drove by on the street. People strolled the slate sidewalks at a leisurely pace enjoying the mild sunny weather.

"Kassie, will you watch for my mother, in case she comes back looking for us?"

Sarah's biggest worry was that her mother would return and find them gone.

Kassie assured her, "I will watch every day."

They let their legs swing back and forth creating a gentle sway on the swing.

"I hope Uncle John doesn't decide to settle in Slate Run."

Sarah put her teacup on a small table near the swing. "That can't happen. Father has the business here and our house too, and his brother and all of you."

Kassie still voiced concern. "But now you will be with Aunt Virginia, and cousins Mason and Janine. What if you don't want to come back?"

"Kassie, I was five years old the last time they came to visit. I have always been with you. Don't forget that Slate Run doesn't have a school. Father knows it will be difficult for me to keep up with my studies on my own. We will come back—" sometimes Sarah had her own doubts, "—I'm almost sure of it." Sarah picked up her teacup again. "Some nights I can't sleep thinking about all I'm leaving behind."

Their feet dangling freely from the swing, they continued watching the people in the street go by.

The night before leaving town, Sarah's thoughts kept her awake. She wished over and over that everything could return to the way it was before mother left.

An hour before dawn Sarah dressed for the trip. Downstairs she saw father in the parlor reading the paper and drinking his coffee. "Good morning, Father. Do I have time to walk by the river for a while?"

He looked up from the paper. "You have about an hour. I have some items to pick up at the office before we leave. If you come home and I'm not here, you will know where I am."

Sarah left through the front gate walking down the sidewalk past Kassie's house. When she was far enough down the street that father wouldn't see her, she took off running toward the river. In the early hours of morning an idea had occurred to her that was impossible to let go. At the river's edge Sarah took the fisherman's footpath, stopping when she arrived at Revival Bible Church. The white paint of the building glowed in the predawn light. The only sound was the Susquehanna River drifting slowly by.

She stared at the steeple. Its cross reached toward the sky. Her pulse was pounding. She felt shame over what her mother had done, at what people would think of her family. She felt anger toward Reverend Claythorn for destroying her family. The thought scared her that everything she was familiar with was slipping away.

Along the banks of the Susquehanna she scooped up a handful of rocks, squeezing them in her tight fists. She thought about her mother's Bible lying open on the foyer floor after father had thrown it against the wall. Was this the emotion that her father felt when he threw it against the wall?

With a loud cry she flung a rock aimed straight toward one of the windows. It shattered loudly into a million sparkling pieces that spread across the rose bed below it. The adrenaline rose up in her along with a feeling of control at having broken the window. She tossed a rock again. One after the other, they flew out of her hand. With each release of a rock she cried out until all of the windows in the church were shattered. Only a few jagged pieces of glass remained in the window frames, clinging at odd angles. She held her now empty fists up to her pounding chest. A feeling of justice rose inside of her. She ran home just as the sun was rising over the mountains.

Uncle Jacob, Aunt Katherine, Elijah, and Kassie were waiting on the front porch when she returned. They brought with them warm muffins and oatmeal cookies for their trip. Kassie cried and hugged Sarah, but Sarah remained dry-eyed, too spent to cry. Their luggage was placed in Uncle Jacob's wagon. He would drive them to the Exchange Hotel where the packer boats were docked.

When the Trinity tower bell struck eight times, they left for the hotel. Williamsport was already in full sunlight; the riverbanks were teeming with people. When they arrived at the hotel the horses for the packer boats were being tethered to the pulleys. Sarah hated the feeling of panic that was overwhelming her as the reality of their departure came upon them. Sarah and Kassie clung to each other again.

Her father gave his brother one last hug then headed toward Sarah. "It's time to go, Sarah." He waited near Kassie and Sarah as they finished hugging.

Kassie wiped her eyes dry. "I'll write you, Sarah—I'll let you know where we are in our studies in school so you don't fall behind. I'll tell you all the news from town." She reached into her pocket for a small bag she gave to Sarah. "Lemon drops for your trip."

Sarah put them in the pocket of her dress. The boats were ready for passengers. Her father helped her to the benches up top. Once everyone was settled in, the horses began to pull on the ropes. The boat gave an initial jerk. They began their journey on the Susquehanna River. Uncle Jacob, Aunt Katherine and Elijah waved goodbye to them.

Kassie ran along the riverbanks, waving. "Bye, Sarah, I love you!"

Sarah waved back. She lost sight of Kassie when the boat came to a bend in the river. She looked up when an audible gasp caught her attention. The boat was passing Revival Bible Church, with all its windows broken. Sarah felt guilt wash over her face. She was sure her face was red, that everyone would know she was the one who had broken the windows. When she looked at her father, he didn't seem to notice the shattered church windows. She reached for his hand. Sarah didn't know what the future held, but she was grateful that she still had her father.

The village of Jersey Shore was home to numerous farms and a large silk mill. Travelers heading into the Pine Creek Gorge often stopped for supplies. Pine Creek flowing south from the gorge met the waters of the Susquehanna River here. A railroad line ran through the village and followed Pine Creek to the lumber towns in upstate Pennsylvania. When Sarah and her father reached Jersey Shore, he unloaded the packer boat with assistance from a gentleman at the hotel where they would be staying. It was early afternoon, so there was enough time for lunch before they headed out for supplies. Sarah found herself excited to see a new town. She had never been outside of Williamsport.

They stopped at a general store where her father bought flour, cornmeal, oats, and coffee. At the Blacksmith shop John purchased a wagon. The Blacksmith recommended a stable two blocks north on Railroad Street where they could purchase a horse.

Five horses were loose in the corral when they arrived. While her father was talking to the liveryman, Sarah stepped on the bottom railing of the corral to watch the horses. Her new boots gave her great traction on the railing. A chestnut stallion came trotting toward her pushing his nose against her sleeve. She reached up to stroke his velvet nose. When he stood still she scratched him behind his chin too. He whinnied and pranced in a circle and came back to nudge her arm again.

The liveryman and her father came around the corner. "I see your daughter has good taste. That chestnut is my most valuable stallion".

The two bickered on a price until both of them felt like they had a good deal. Before the purchase was completed Sarah decided the horse would be named "Duke." Her father made arrangements to pick up Duke in the morning. That night they slept soundly for the first time since Mary left.

At dawn her father walked to the stable to get Duke, and then rode over to the Blacksmith shop to get the wagon. The supplies from the general store had been delivered to the hotel the night before. He loaded the wagon while Sarah bathed before their long journey into the gorge. Sarah's hair was still damp as they sat in the dining hall eating a warm breakfast. After eating, her father took their belongings from the room while Sarah purchased sandwiches for the trip.

Everything outside was wet with dew; the air was damp and foggy. There was no one here to say goodbye to so they left Jersey Shore quietly, crossing a bridge under which the waters of Pine Creek flowed into the Susquehanna River. They sat on the bumpy buckboard seat with Duke pulling them along the road that would lead them to their new home.

CHAPTER 6

The Journey North

Sarah and her father began their winding journey into the Pine Creek Gorge. Sarah pulled her jacket snug around her neck against the cool mountain air. She could only see a few feet around her, which made everything feel mysterious. The woods were so thick with trees there were areas in which no light ever reached the forest floor. Where there was light, the ground was covered with blueberry bushes, laurel, and vines hanging down from tree branches. Boughs of green sheltered their path overhead; fallen leaves coated the road below. Often, the road would look like it was going to end at the base of a mountain, then it would take a sharp turn crossing over a bridge to the other side of Pine Creek. Around each bend the mountains closed in behind them. Sarah tried to capture each scene in her mind so she could sketch it from memory.

It was a strange feeling to be going so far away from home. She reached over and brushed her hand against an oak branch hanging near the path; droplets of water raced to the ground. Her father suddenly stopped the wagon. At first she thought she had done something wrong, but he was pointing to the hillside ahead of them.

He whispered. "Stay quiet so we don't startle them."

Sarah quickly drew in her breath when she saw a mother bear and two very large cubs slowly sauntering down the mountain toward the road. The bears paid them no mind as they lumbered over rocks and fallen trees. The mother bear stopped often to monitor the progress of her two cubs. The hillside was steep, causing one of the cubs to slide on a patch of wet leaves. It made a little squeal. The mother bear continued on. When the bears reached the road, one of the cubs briefly raised its head toward them, and then followed its mother and sibling down the steep riverbank. Her father stayed still long enough to make sure the movement of the wagon wouldn't alarm the mother bear.

It was the first time Sarah had encountered a bear. "I can't wait to write Kassie about this! She won't believe it!"

Her father snapped the reigns to begin their journey again. "I haven't crossed paths with a wild animal for a number of years. Don't ever approach a mother bear; they won't hesitate to attack to protect their young."

Sarah had watched the bears closely. "I noticed how she kept looking back at her young ones."

After meeting the wild bears, they were silent again. When the sun finally burned through the fog, the azure sky arched over them the rest of the day. The mountains rose abruptly from the valley floor, reaching a thousand feet or more. They passed a small town every few miles, compressed into a small valley in between the mountains that hemmed them in. She understood now why it was called a gorge.

The sun was high over the mountains when they stopped at a spring. Dusty from the trip, they splashed fresh water over their faces. The cold water refreshed Sarah's skin. They ate a lunch of sandwiches in a clearing of grass where the sun was shining through the trees. Robins and Blue jays were singing in great numbers, fluttering around from one tree to another. Her father rested on a large rock with a view of the valley. Sarah explored the forest nearby wishing her mother were there to see the beautiful mountains. After an hour they resumed their journey.

As darkness began to fall they came into the little village of Ramsey. Multiple streams flowed loudly off the mountain into Pine Creek. They parked their wagon outside of the village near the creek. Exhausted, they ate a cold dinner before crawling into the beds they made with quilts from home. Sarah stared at the stars for a while, amazed at how many she could see, and then she rolled over onto her side and closed her eyes.

The next day, they crossed a large wooden bridge into Jersey Mills, stopping briefly at the post office to see how far they still had to go. They were told they would reach their destination the following night. That evening they camped along the creek bank in the village of Cammal. The water was shallow and wide, flowing noisily over the creek rocks. Tomorrow they would see their new home.

Her father built a fire that shone bright against the black wilderness that surrounded them. Sarah was remembering the article she had read about the man who had been dragged away by a panther. She pulled herself closer to the fire to guard against a surprise attack from a wild animal. "Father, can you hear a panther when it's sneaking up on you?"

His answer frightened her. "No. They are like a cat, creeping silently before they pounce." He quickly added, "But they don't like fire."

Her shoulders relaxed some.

Her father took something from his pocket. "And they hate the sound of a harmonica."

He played his harmonica for a while, the sound echoing off the mountains. She sat looking at the stars while he played songs. She felt safe with her father close by.

After a few tunes he tapped the harmonica on his leg. Reaching forward, he stirred the remaining coals in the fire. Small embers floated up, disappearing into the darkness above them. Sarah was amazed at the number of stars dotting across the sky.

Her father was looking at them too. "I haven't taken the time to look up at the stars in a long time."

He took a stick in his hand and drew an imaginary line across the sky, following a thick path of stars. "That patch of stars is called the Milky Way; it's a patch of stars so numerous that from here, it looks like spilled milk."

He gazed into the fire again. "Your mother loved looking at the stars. One night, before you were born, she woke me up in the middle of the night to drive out of town to a large field to see a comet shower she had read about. She packed up a blanket, made hot cocoa, even cookies."

He smiled. "We sat in a field for hours before a single comet raced across the sky, quickly fizzling out of sight."

Sarah wanted to hear more. "Father, how did you meet Mother?"

She could tell by the expression on his face he was surprised at the question. He was quiet for a moment. It seemed like he was searching for the memory.

"I haven't thought about those days in a long time." Her father filled his tin with liquid from the kettle resting above the fire. "I met your mother when I was eleven. My family moved from Dushore to Williamsport in the middle of the school year. On my first day at school I didn't have a slate to write on. She offered to share hers with me until I had one."

Sarah had never heard this story before. "Were you friends after that?"

"She didn't like me, but I was smitten with her. The best way I knew how to show my love for her was to steal her hair ribbons and chase her with spiders."

"Father! She hates spiders!"

"She didn't talk to me after that. Uncle Jacob tried to warn me, but I didn't listen." He put his coffee tin on a rock next to him.

All that remained of the fire were a few smoldering embers.

"I'll tell you one more story—then it's time for bed. Tomorrow we'll see our new home and reunite with Aunt Virginia and her family."

He told Sarah about hunting with his brother when they were younger. With the fire so low, the darkness crept in closer. A few times, Sarah heard a twig snap behind her or the rustling of leaves in the woods. Her father paused and she caught him looking at something to her right.

Out of the corner of her sight, she saw a flash of white. She jumped up when she realized a skunk had come close to the fire, right next to her! Against better judgment she ran toward her father. They both rushed into the little tent near the wagon. Sarah was shaking from the close call.

Her father whispered close to her ear, "Did you see how close he was? I thought he was going to walk right over your shoe."

Sarah had a sudden thought. "What about Duke?"

"If the skunk was going to spray I think it would have happened when you jumped up and ran to the tent. I don't think there would be any reason for him to bother Duke."

They both laughed quietly with relief at their escape. Plates clanged by the fire pit as the skunk inspected them for food. Exhausted, Sarah and her father were both asleep before the skunk left.

Sarah woke up the next morning to the sound of soft munching on the other side of the tent. She was afraid the skunk was still there. Her father was peering out the tent door and he motioned for her to come over quietly. Just outside the tent were a dozen elk grazing on the grass. One of the elk had a very large rack of antlers. He raised his head, making a loud raspy bugle call. When her father finally stood up outside the tent, the herds of elk moved further down the field keeping watchful glances on them until he and Sarah were headed down the road.

Early that evening they arrived in the village of Slate Run. A thick cloud hung low between the high mountains, making it feel like dusk. The damp air clung to their skin like a cool blanket. They drove over the railroad tracks passing a small train station with a long wooden platform. Just north of the station were two small homes and a general store with a tall false front rising up an extra story above the store. The post office and boarding house sat next to each other, south of the train station. Sarah and her father crossed the creek on a narrow bridge just north of which Sarah could see a splash dam spanning the river. She knew this was used by the woodhicks to control water flow as they moved lumber down the creek in the spring. The church sat directly in the path of the bridge, the parsonage behind it.

Her father pointed to the right of the bridge, "Aunt Virginia's place is over there."

She looked down a road to the right of the bridge. A large green yard reached from the bridge, all the way down to the creek and far across to the hotel's front porch, which wrapped around two sides of the building. The hotel sat against the mountainside at the edge of the forest. When they neared the property, a lady seated in a rocking chair on the front porch stood up. Sarah recognized Aunt Virginia as she ran to the road hollering for everyone to come.

A boy about seven years old was running behind Sarah's aunt. Sarah guessed it was her cousin Mason. Clinging to a porch post was little five-year-old Janine who followed the commotion with her unseeing eyes. Janine had been blind since birth.

Her aunt was much shorter than her brother but had the same brunette hair and face. She hugged her brother in a tight embrace. "John! It's been too long!"

Mason looked at the cousin his mother had told him about. He was observing her face and hair when he made a loud decision, "Mother, she's pretty!"

This made her aunt pull away from her father. She put a gentle hand on Mason's shoulder. "Mason, this is your cousin Sarah."

Mason reached his hand out toward Sarah. "Nice to meet you cousin Sarah."

Her aunt continued the introduction. "And this," she directed his attention to her brother, "is Uncle John."

Mason reached a hand up to Uncle John in greeting too, "Nice to meet you, Uncle John."

Uncle Harold came around the corner of the hotel from the direction of the creek. "I was hoping you would make it here before dark!" He was short and round. He took off his hat and shook Sarah's hand first. His grasp was strong. "Sarah, it is good to see you after all these years. You are so grown-up looking."

He gave his brother-in-law a huge hug then slapped him on the back. "John, it is good to see you again too. How was the trip—any problems?"

A cry from the porch brought all of their attention to Janine who had been left out of all the greetings.

Sarah was the first one to reach her, putting her hands over Janine's. "Janine, I'm your cousin Sarah. I think we will be best friends."

Janine let her grip go from the porch post. Reaching forward, she put both her hands on Sarah's face. Janine smiled with her whole face. Sarah sat on the top step so Janine could crawl into her lap.

Aunt Virginia led the group to the porch. "Harold will show you the way to your place. May I send some dinner home with you?" Sarah wished they could visit longer. Her father must have been thinking the same thing. "I wish we had more time to visit."

Aunt Virginia reassured her brother. "John, you will not regret it when you get a good night's rest. We have tomorrow for visiting, and—"

He raised an eyebrow at her. "And?"

She smiled at him. "You will need your rest because most of the town is coming to meet the newcomers at dinner tomorrow."

"Most of the town?"

"Maybe thirty people. It's the way we do things here. Everyone knows everyone."

Within twenty minutes they were ready to go. Uncle Harold rode his horse ahead of them to a road toward the mountain that passed by the church and parsonage. On the right, the field ran up to a narrow line of trees separating the field from the parsonage. To the left, the field ran toward homes along the river, where she could see a cluster of buildings. Uncle Harold pointed out the woodhick camp and James B. Weed & Company Sawmill in the cluster of buildings. The Pennsylvania Joint Land Company, where her father would work, was on the other side of the river near the post office and boarding house.

The road ended in a small overgrown yard in which sat a small wood cabin with a copper roof, weathered green. A few feet from the cabin toward the mountain were a small barn and a corral.

Her uncle looked surprised at the condition of the place. "I apologize, John. We haven't been able to get away from the hotel."

Before leaving for home he helped carry the luggage and supplies into the cabin. Her father put Duke in the barn. Sarah helped by bringing their satchels and some of the food supplies inside. The front room contained an iron cook stove and a small table with two chairs. Opposite the kitchen a rocking chair sat near the fireplace. Two small rooms contained a single bed frame and a single window. The cabin felt empty even with all their belongings inside. Sarah yawned. Her father lit a small lantern on the table. Tonight they would sleep on the floor next to the fireplace with the blankets from home.

Leia

"Mother" by Sarah Richardson

CHAPTER 7

Leia

On her knees, in the middle of the garden, Leia snapped pea pods from their stalks. "Leia," she repeated the name silently several times during the day as if hearing it for the first time. She remembered her mother telling her as a young girl, "Leia means loyal." Now that she was with her mother memories were returning to her in fragments.

Her mother called from the other end of the garden, near the cornstalks. "Are there enough peas for dinner?"

Leia brushed a strand of hair off her warm face. It was hot for September. She reached for another pod tucked away near the bottom of the plant. "Yes, but this might be the last harvest of peas this year. They are small and sparse, mother."

Caroline walked toward her, putting two corncobs in the basket sitting between the 2 rows of pea shrubs. When she stood, she reached her hands around to the small of her aching back.

A woolly worm making its way across a leaf on the shrub startled Leia. She picked up the furry-looking creature to examine the auburn and black bands of color covering its body. "Most of the wooly worms I see this year have more black than auburn. Do you remember what that means mother?"

Caroline looked over at her. "You still believe that old tale?"

Leia rehearsed the quote. "More black and you have a hard winter. More auburn and winter is mild."

Caroline was still pressing her hands into the small of her back. "I hope we don't have a hard winter."

Leia was examining the worm closely, remembering something. "Do you know who taught me about wooly worms?"

Caroline was quiet.

Leia continued, "Do you remember the day the railroad man came to interview father for a job?"

Leia noticed her mother looked away, toward the creek. "I hoped you had forgotten about that day but then—" she placed a bonnet on her head "—how could you forget?"

"Father told me about the stripes of the woolly worm the day before, while we were walking in the woods. The next day he dressed in his best suit because an important man from the railroad was coming for a visit. He told me to stay outside until the guest left the house."

Caroline closed her eyes. "I was hanging laundry outside. I foolishly thought I could watch you while I hung the laundry, even though you were five years old and very curious."

Leia continued, "I wandered over by some fallen trees at the edge of the property where I found a woolly worm with large auburn stripes." She examined the creature she held now, watching it crawl across the back of her hand. "I was so excited to show father my discovery I forgot about being told to stay outside."

Caroline sat next to Leia. "I tried to holler out for you to stop, but you were so quick."

"I ran inside tracking mud across the kitchen floor and burst through the parlor door. The railroad man was finishing the interview. The door hit him in the arm as he was standing up.

'Father, father! Look what I found!'

I held the worm up for inspection, thinking father's friend might also be interested in seeing the worm. The man acted as if he did not see me at all as he took his hat from the arm of his chair.

'Good day, Mr. Oakley', and he quickly left. After father saw the man out, he rushed over to me."

Caroline's voice was shaky with emotion. "Leia, I have never forgiven myself for not going inside after you. I knew what he was capable of, and I didn't save you from him."

Leia didn't look at her mother as she continued. She pulled a long strand of grass through her fingers, feeling its soft edges against her skin. "I was so frightened by how quickly he grabbed me that I couldn't catch my breath. I dropped the woolly worm onto the floor as he slammed me down into one of the kitchen chairs. He started slapping me across the face—my insides were trembling from fear. He continued hitting me; I kept myself distracted by watching the woolly worm crawl across the kitchen floor toward the door. My mouth was filling with blood, and my eyes were closing up from the swelling, but I didn't cry. The only sound I remember were the horrible things father was yelling as he hit me.

'You stupid child! I needed that job! You did that on purpose, didn't you?'

He bent down to yell in my face, 'You are the most worthless child I know!'" Leia continued, "I thought at one point I was going to die. Then he stopped as suddenly as he had begun. He walked out of the kitchen door, stepping on the wooly worm on his way out. Only then did I cry out loud. That is when I began to hate him."

Tears were spilling over her mother's face. "I am sorry, Leia."

Leia reached for her mother's shaking hands; she was too overcome to speak anymore.

"Leia, I was afraid when I saw what he had done to you, his own daughter—there were many nights I stayed awake—trying to figure out how to run away from him."

Someone calling to them from the house interrupted their conversation.

"Mrs. Oakley?"

A large black man was standing at the front door. He raised his hand to knock again, but paused in mid-air when he saw them in the garden.

Caroline waved toward the man. "Jeremiah!"

Leia still felt the fog of the memory on her. She watched Jeremiah come toward them in great strides. He was at least six feet tall.

"Leia, I want you to meet my friend, Jeremiah. He and his wife, Ruby, have been a great help to me."

Jeremiah smiled the kind of smile that involves the whole face.

"Jeremiah, this is my daughter, Leia."

Leia could tell Jeremiah was surprised at meeting Caroline's daughter. "It is nice to meet you Leia. My wife Ruby will want to meet you too. We are good friends of Miss Caroline."

Leia could tell by her mother's expression that Jeremiah was a very good friend.

"Jeremiah, is your family well?"

"Yes, Miss Caroline. I'm headed into town to get some flour for Ruby. I stopped by to see if you need anything."

"Thank you, but not today." Caroline stood up, taking the basket of vegetables into her arms. "Would you care for some tea before heading into town?"

"No, I'm under strict orders to return home immediately so Ruby can finish making bread. If you don't mind, I'll be on my way."

"Good day Jeremiah. Please tell Ruby I have some extra corn in the garden if she needs any."

"Thank you. I will."

He tipped his hat to them and continued his walk to town.

Leia walked to some milkweed at the edge of the garden to release the woolly worm on one of the large leaves. She was comforted by the fact that this woolly worm was safe from harm.

Inside the kitchen, Caroline pumped water into the large sink in order to wash the peas. Leia sliced bread for lunch and put apple butter on the table.

"Mother, what have you told people about me? Did Jeremiah know you had a daughter?"

Caroline shook the colander of peas to release the extra water. She poured the pods onto a cloth in the middle of the table.

"People know my husband was killed in a railroad accident, and that you went missing that same day. They know I have never stopped praying you would come back home."

Leia spread apple butter on a slice of bread. "I don't know why I ran away the day of father's accident. An older couple, Lillian and Graham Dalton, took me in when I told them my family was killed in a fire. I never gave thought to how much pain I was causing you when I chose to forget the past. Did you ever give up hope I would return?"

"I waited for five years, in the old house, haunted by the memories of everything that happened there." she paused to snap a few pea pods before continuing. "This home is where I grew up. When my parents passed away, I moved here to start a new life in Trout Run. It was very difficult for me to move away not knowing where you were—How did you find me here?"

"When I was pregnant with Sarah—" Leia suddenly realized she hadn't yet told her mother she had a granddaughter "—I hired a detective to find you. The Daltons had recently passed away; I was beginning to remember things I had long forgotten." Leia was sitting with her elbows on the farm table, her head resting in her hands. "It only took a month for the detective to find you. I rode the stagecoach here, staying one night at the hotel, but I was too afraid to see you after all the years that had gone by, so I left. I thought it might be better if you believed I was dead. That was fourteen years ago."

Looking up, Leia noticed the large knuckles on her mother's hands, the pronounced wrinkles in her skin. So much time had been lost between her and her mother. Her mother's work-worn hands paused in their task; her eyes were watery as she looked at her Leia.

"What made you come back this time?"

Leia barely knew how to explain her situation. "I left my family. I—I wasn't the kind of wife and mother they needed."

Her mother reached her hand toward Leia, "Is that what they told you?"

"No mother—I'm so ashamed." Leia looked down at her hands in her apron. "I betrayed my husband—my good husband—my daughter!"

Her mother's voice came to her with sadness not judgment, "You have believed the lie your father told you."

Leia was shocked at her mother's response. "Lie?"

"The lie that you are not worth anything."

"But mother—the things I have done prove what father said about me. I have often wondered if it would have been better if I had never been born."

"Leia, don't say such a thing! The things you have done or what you have been told does not define your worth. God loves you. He did not make a mistake when you were born."

Leia was looking into her mother's eyes. She was feeling overwhelmed with the loss of time between her mother and her, and the complete unraveling of her family in Williamsport.

"Leia, I never stopped loving you, never stopped praying I would see you again."

Leia let her mother's words go deep inside her to a place that had long needed healing. It was a while before they began snapping open the pea pods again.

CHAPTER 8

Country Living

The next two days were sunny and unusually warm. Sarah and her father worked at getting the cabin and corral livable. The mattresses on the beds had to be filled with hay. Sarah held the bed bags open while her father stuffed them full with hay purchased at the general store. It was a messy job that made them sneeze continuously. By the time they were done, they were covered in a fine dusting of hay that made their skin itch. It was her father's idea to take a quick swim in the creek. They found a large rock that sat above a deep pool in the creek. He jumped off the rock first, splashing down into the water right next to Sarah who had cautiously waded into the cool waters.

"Father!"

When it was her turn to jump, she pulled her knees to her chest, reached her hands around her ankles and dropped into the water with a great splash. As soon as her feet brushed the bottom of the creek, she straightened her legs to propel her body to the surface of the water. Just as she took a large breath of air her father splashed down into the water right next to her again. When he came to the surface, she grabbed him tightly around the neck. He spun around in a fast circle. It was difficult for her to hang on tight because she was laughing so hard. Finally exhausted, they walked the path home. Sarah could not remember a time in her life when she had so much fun with her father. She wished Mother were here with them.

CHAPTER 9

Fall

The colors of the forest changed under dark October skies and freezing temperatures. Bright hues of yellow and red contrasted with the green hemlock trees on the surrounding mountains. Sarah knew it would not be long before the woodhicks stripped these hills of their lumber. On days when the weather was dry, she drew pictures of the hills so someday she could show her children how things used to be.

Once her father started his work at the Pennsylvania Joint Land and Lumber Company, he was rarely home. Most of Sarah's meals were eaten at the hotel where she spent a lot of time with her aunt. It was in the lonely hours, brushing Duke or walking in the woods, when she thought about her mother. She often wondered why her mother left them or if her mother still loved her.

It was only a matter of weeks before she would be confined indoors by the cold weather. After brushing Duke she packed a lunch for a hike. Behind the hotel she followed the path of a little spring half way up the mountain before she reached a deer path that continued to the top of the mountain. The steep hillside rose abruptly from the valley floor. Wet leaves and pine needles were slippery underfoot. Often Sarah would grab an exposed root or tree trunk to keep herself from sliding down the mountain. Near the top, a rock rose up thirty feet from the forest floor rising above the trees. From this rock she could see the river and the town far below her. It was a quiet place, high above the sound of the sawmill that cut 100,000 board feet of lumber a day. To the north of town the lumbering was beginning to make a scar on the forests. Woodhicks had begun clear-cutting the trees, leaving only stumps sticking up from the ground. The exposed forest floor was barren and brown. Behind her at the top of the mountain, she could see smoke rising from a chimney, curling up into the sky from someone's cabin.

Leaving the rock to venture further up the mountain she found a meadow surrounded by hemlock trees. Under the subdued light of thick clouds she took her backpack off, laid out a small blanket, drawing pad, and a schoolbook. She looked at her copy of *Civil Government*. She thumbed through the pages finally deciding she would draw after reading two chapters in the book. She didn't want to find out she had fallen behind in her studies when she returned to school in Williamsport. It was difficult studying on her own; she missed sitting next to Kassie in school and wondered who was sitting at her desk now. She leaned against a rock at the edge of the blanket to read, almost falling asleep by the time she finished the second chapter. Civil Government was not her favorite subject.

She placed the schoolbook inside her satchel. The woods were quiet. Drawing pad finally in hand, she sketched the forest around her, soaking in the peacefulness. She was so quiet while drawing that a squirrel running down a nearby tree trunk was startled by her presence. It chatted loudly at her, ran back up the tree across a branch, and on to another tree. Sarah was amused at the surprised squirrel.

Clouds drifted apart, allowing a window of sunshine to light the meadow. She paused her drawing to enjoy the warmth of the sun on her skin. A soft breeze stirred fallen leaves into twisting circles along the ground. Watching the leaves she was overcome with the memory of her mother hanging out laundry on a day similar to this. She could see the clean linens snapping gently in the breeze, colorful leaves falling in dancing patterns around her mother. Sarah often caught her mother gazing up into the blue skies, sometimes with a far-off look. Now she wondered if that had been a glimpse of unhappiness.

She started to draw her mother. The side of her mother's face began to take shape on the paper, her mother's hair in a bun with wavy tendrils coming loose in the breeze. A rustling in the leaves near the edge of the blanket startled her. She looked with frightened eyes into the forest.

Leaves rustled nearby again.

She reached up for the string around her neck having previously forgotten about the bell that her father had given her to wear in the woods. She was supposed to ring it occasionally so wildlife would know she was there. Sarah tugged on the string and jiggled the bell to sound an alert.

The rustling stopped.

She quietly put the drawing pad and pencils down on the blanket. The rustling started again distinctly closer and heading her way. Sarah was breathing quicker now. She looked into the forest but couldn't see anything. Closer and closer the sound came. She could see the leaves and twigs on a laurel bush moving. Sarah wondered how much noise a panther would make.

She hollered out into the forest. "Go away!"

Sarah rang her bell again, and thought about running but couldn't get her legs to move underneath her. She screamed when a skunk suddenly appeared from beneath a shrub and walked onto her blanket. The sight of Sarah equally scared the skunk. It sprayed a healthy dose of stink from its tail. Sarah ran blindly spitting and gagging on the fumes before she slammed into the side of something that caused her to fall down hard on her backside.

When she looked up it was into the face of a horse. High up on the horse sat a young man plugging his nose and looking quite amused. She was embarrassed that someone had seen her predicament.

"You looked pretty funny running into the side of my horse and—" The boy pulled a hanky out of his saddlebag, which he tied around his nose, "—you smell awful!"

He reached a hand toward her. "Can I offer you a ride home?"

Sarah was looking up at him speechless, irritated at his laughing at her.

When she didn't respond he continued, "My name is Matthew. I live with my family on top of this mountain."

Sarah was unsure what to do.

Matthew looked into the surrounding woods. "It's going to be dark soon. Please let me give you a ride home."

Sarah knew she wouldn't make it out of the forest before dark. No matter how irritated she was, she needed help to get home safe. "I have to get my satchel."

Matthew followed her the short distance to the meadow. The skunk was nowhere in sight. She gathered up her items, all of which smelled terrible, and put them in her satchel. It was disheartening for her to see everything ruined.

Matthew pulled her up onto the saddle behind him. Apologizing for her smell, she held on to him for the ride home. "I'm afraid you're going to stink too by the time you get home. I'm sorry."

Speaking through the hanky he told her, "It's fine. This is the most adventure I have had since my dog ran into a skunk after we moved to the ranch last year."

Sarah was curious. "What happened to the dog?"

"He smelled for months."

Sarah could tell that he was laughing at her again. "I'm going to smell like this until spring?"

Matthew continued to have spontaneous bouts of laughter as they rode down the mountainside. Sarah finally smacked him on the back. It was bothering her that he was so amused. He became apologetic, "Sorry, I keep picturing you running blindly into the side of my horse."

Matthew was silent the rest of the ride home. He dropped her off at the barn. As he turned his horse toward home, he tipped his hat to Sarah. "In case we should meet again, what should I call you? I don't want to refer to you as skunk girl."

"Sarah Richardson. And your last name?"

"Stephens, Matthew Stephens."

He headed back up the mountain.

Sarah called after him. "Thank you, Matthew!" Although he had been too amused, he had helped her.

He didn't look back but waved his hat over his head as he rode away. Sarah put her bag in the barn before running across the field to the hotel. Her aunt would know what to do.

Not wanting to go inside the kitchen she knocked on the door. Mason came to the door first, took a whiff and ran away plugging his nose and yelling.

"Mother, Sarah's at the door and she stinks!"

Aunt Virginia brought a large tub out to the horse barn. Sarah placed her clothes in a barrel. While Sarah soaked in the tub, her aunt rubbed a paste of hydrogen peroxide, soap, and baking soda through Sarah's hair. When her aunt poured water over her head the skunk smell was strong again.

"Aunt Virginia, do I smell any better?"

"Yes, but every time you wet you hair, for a while, it will reactivate the skunk smell."

Sarah reached for a lock of her hair to smell. It was better, but it still made her nose wrinkle.

Aunt Virginia tried to encourage her. "It's better than it was, Sarah." She laid out some clothing for her niece. "I think you're about my height now. These clothes will be baggy, but at least you can get home."

Sarah talked to her aunt while she changed in a nearby stall. "Will I be able to help you in the kitchen tomorrow?"

"You will be fine in the kitchen. I can't have you serving food for a while though. Where did you run into the skunk?"

"I was near the top of the mountain. A boy named Matthew Stephens happened to be riding past after I got sprayed. He brought me home."

"That was nice of him, especially because he will be a bit smelly too."

Sarah stepped out of the stall looking down at the baggy clothes she now wore. Sarah told her aunt about Matthew laughing at her. "He thought the whole incident was quite amusing."

"Sarah, I'm honestly having a difficult time not laughing too. The way you describe running through the woods without knowing where you were going and bumping into Matthew's horse is really quite funny. Imagine him riding through a quiet forest and coming upon a smelly girl running crazily through the woods."

Sarah looked thoughtful. "I guess it would have been pretty funny to see; it's embarrassing that he witnessed me in that way."

Her aunt brushed Sarah's hair to loosen stray bits of baking soda. "The Stephens' family owns a forty-acre ranch on top of the mountain. It's the only place trees are safe from the axe of the woodhicks. Mr. Stephens comes down occasionally for supplies, but I rarely see Matthew."

Sarah could see that it was dark outside. "I'm worried father will be home, wondering where I am."

"Uncle Harold went to the lumber company before dark to tell him what happened. Mason went with him. He was very excited to tell your father what happened."

"I won't ever live this down, will I?"

"Not until something more exciting happens. Uncle Harold will take you home."

Sarah hugged her aunt goodbye. When Uncle Harold helped her into the wagon, she looked up at the mountain searching for light from the Stephens Ranch but the clouds were hanging too low over the mountain. Her uncle tied a hanky over his nose in spite of her cleaning. She smiled; it was hard to ignore the fact that today had been adventurous and quite humorous. It was a good day after all.

CHAPTER 10

Life Goes On

The next morning rain was drizzling down in a fine mist. Sarah found her satchel in the barn. Emptying all of its contents onto the floor, she looked at the sketches of squirrels, trees, pine creek, and her mother. Not knowing what else to do, to rid the papers of the smell, she ran a rope from a hook on one end of the stall to a hook where the lantern hung at the other end of the stall. She clipped each drawing to the rope with a wooden clothespin, hoping the fresh mountain air and the smell of hay, over time, would dissolve the odor.

Sarah stroked Duke behind his ear fearing he would protest at how she smelled, but he nudged her with his nose. From the open barn door she could see the wet fields. On rainy days in Williamsport, her mother would warm up the house by baking pies or bread. Sarah would help her mother by crimping the edges of the pies or punching the rising bread dough. She reached up to scratch Duke behind his ears.

"Why did mother think she had to leave?"

Sarah wished things could be back to normal. She filled Duke's bag with oats. Smoke was rising from the chimney at the Pennsylvania Joint Land and Lumber Company across the creek where her father spent his days. When he was home he looked tired and older than he had in Williamsport. She wished there were more days like the one she and her father spent swimming in the creek.

It would soon be time for her aunt to start preparing lunch for the woodhicks, so Sarah decided to make her way to the hotel. At the bridge she stopped to look over the edge at the swiftly moving water. She dropped a single round rock into the creek to watch it quickly disappear under the brown water.

Above the sound of the rapids, Sarah heard yelling coming from across the creek. She could see Mrs. Jensen standing at the edge of the creek bank, behind the boarding house, emptying glass bottles into the water. Mr. Jensen stumbled around the side of the house yelling slurred obscenities at her with each step he took. When he saw the liquid from the last bottle being emptied into the creek, he fell to the ground whimpering like a child, even curling into a little ball. Mrs. Jensen tried to drag him back to the house, looking around to see if anyone was watching. Two men from the boarding house carried him inside for her.

Sarah remembered the first time she met Mrs. Jensen. It was their second evening in town when Aunt Virginia hosted a dinner at the hotel to introduce them to everyone. Mr. Jensen slept through most of the dinner in a porch chair. Sarah overheard one of the woodhicks joking about him having too much to drink again. Mrs. Jensen joined them for dinner but didn't say much all evening.

Sarah recalled a moment during dinner when Mrs. Jensen, who sat in a seat across from her, reached for the saltshaker in the center of the table. Her loose sleeve caught on the edge of the table, pulling her sleeve up on her arm. Sarah stared at the large bruise it revealed. When Mrs. Jensen noticed Sarah's stare she looked down at her arm alarmed at what was showing. She quickly pulled the sleeve down and abruptly left the table. It wasn't until now that Sarah thought anything about what she had seen. She continued walking to the hotel. Sarah let herself into the kitchen when she arrived.

"Sarah!" It was Mason that called out to her first, causing her aunt to look up from the wood-topped island where she was rolling out bread dough.

Janine and Mason were seated at a small table and chairs Uncle Harold had built for them. They were playing with extra pie dough. Mason was making a wagon. Janine was squishing the dough between her fingers, laughing. "Sawah?" Janine's blind eyes drifted in her direction.

"Mason, Janine!" Sarah stepped near the small table. "What are my cousins up to on this rainy day?"

Janine was reaching her arms in the direction of her cousin's voice. Sarah lifted her on to her hip. Janine snuggled her head against Sarah's neck. Mason ran over to hug Sarah's legs. Aunt Virginia was smiling while she continued rolling the dough flat.

"Sorry if I'm interrupting anything, Aunt Virginia. With the rain, I wasn't sure what else to do today. Can I help you in the kitchen?"

Her aunt folded the rolled out dough in half and punched it down to remove air bubbles. She answered Sarah while she sprinkled a thin layer of flour over the dough. "I would love the extra help and your company Sarah." She turned her attention to Mason and Janine. "You two go back to playing with the dough. Sarah and I have dinner to prepare."

Sarah put Janine back down in her chair and placed a fresh clump of dough in the child's hands.

Aunt Virginia wiped her hands against her apron. "There is an apron by the pantry you can wear." She motioned toward a large pot on the stove. "Take a ladle from over the stove and stir the stew. Then go into the pantry where you will find a jar of cream ready for churning."

Sarah jumped right into the tasks, happy to work on something she knew how to do.

"You smell better today," her aunt remarked.

Sarah reddened a little at the mention of the skunk incident. She could see Mason at the small table, talking to his sister, fingers pinched over his nose. Janine was giggling. It was obvious they were discussing her encounter with the skunk.

Aunt Virginia noticed them too. "Mason couldn't wait to tell all the woodhicks who came for breakfast today about you and the skunk. Everyone knows about it now."

Sarah stirred the stew and smiled. "I can finally see the humor in it."

They both returned to the tasks at hand. Sarah thought it was interesting to watch the butter separate from the cream while she churned it with a wide paddle. The butter clung to the sides of the ceramic crock leaving the cream in the middle, which would be used for recipes. She stopped the motion of the paddle briefly, her arms tired.

Aunt Virginia was placing four loaves of bread into the oven. "You came to help in the kitchen, Sarah; was there anything else you needed?"

Sarah was always amazed at her aunt's insightfulness. "Actually—" She took a moment to organize her thoughts. "Winter isn't that far away, and I'm realizing that father and I aren't ready to make it through the winter. I don't know how to can food or preserve meat—mother always stocked the pantry. The supplies we brought with us on the wagon will be gone before Christmas—" Sarah paused, "—I want to talk to father about it, but he's gone all day and looks too tired by the time he is home. I don't want to bother him but I'm afraid—"

Aunt Virginia stopped her. "Don't worry anymore about it. I know how to help."

"Oh thank you, Aunt Virginia." She ran to hug her aunt around the waist and glanced down at her aunt's belly, which was sticking out more than usual.

Aunt Virginia put a finger up to her lips, glancing toward Janine and Mason at the same time. She whispered the news softly to Sarah, "They don't know yet. I'm expecting sometime in March."

Sarah quietly jumped in place. "How exciting! Aunt Virginia, I can be here every day to help in the kitchen."

Aunt Virginia smiled. "You can help anytime you like Sarah, but don't feel like you have to. I will be fine. Now back to helping you out.

I will finish the stew for lunch. If you go into the parlor, you will find a pencil and paper on one of the tables; grab them and come back into the kitchen."

Sarah did as she was told then sat in a wooden chair near the pantry. Over the course of the next half hour her aunt helped her make a list of supplies that she and her father would need before winter.

"A train still arrives in town every day this time of year, which means a delivery comes often for the general store. You won't have any trouble getting the items you need."

Sarah looked at the long list. "What is father going to think when he sees this long list?" Sarah put the list in her coat pocket.

"Trust me, I know my brother; he will be relieved we made it."

Aunt Virginia sliced warm bread from the oven, placing each slice in baskets for the tables in the dining room. Woodhicks began filing in to buy a warm lunch. Sarah held the bowls as her aunt filled them with venison stew. She helped run the steaming bowls out to the tables, which were already stocked with crocks of buttermilk and fresh butter. The men devoured more food than she imagined a human could ever eat. She began to wonder if they would have enough to feed all the men, but her aunt had been doing this long enough to know how much to make.

When Sarah saw her father come in she brought him lunch. "Hello, Father."

He seemed stooped over with weariness, but glad to see her.

"I'm helping Aunt Virginia out today."

"That's thoughtful of you to help your Aunt in the kitchen."

He paused. Sarah thought he was going to say something else, but he didn't, so she continued serving the customers while keeping a watchful eye on her father. Near the end of lunch, Aunt Virginia sat with her brother for a while. Sarah could tell she was having a serious talk with him.

Sometime later in the afternoon the rain stopped. Aunt Virginia put Janine on the front porch to play. Mason went to the creek to throw rocks into the water. As they cleaned the kitchen, they heard Janine giggling on the porch. Out of curiosity Sarah and her aunt decided it was time to check on the kids. When they reached Janine, she put her little hands up to show them a tiny turtle squirming in her palms. She giggled every time its little legs squirmed against her skin.

"Mason *gabe* me baby *tutle*".

Aunt Virginia took Janine's hands into her own. "And so he did."

The turtle was no more than an inch in size. Sarah recognized the rough markings on the shell of the turtle from those she had seen along the Susquehanna River in Williamsport. "Aunt Virginia, I think it's a snapping turtle."

Aunt Virginia bent down again to look closer. "I think you are right. It's a wonder there are any left with the way the lumber companies dredge the creek bottoms during the spring drives." Her aunt held Janine's hands together, watchful that the turtle didn't fall.

Sarah wondered where her cousin was. "Where's Mason?"

As soon as she spoke the words they heard Mason yell out to them. "Over here, mother. Come look!"

Mason was belly down on the ground staring over the edge of a freshly dug mound of dirt. Aunt Virginia carried Janine and the little turtle to where Mason was. The large hole in the middle of the mound was full of broken eggshells from which the baby turtles had hatched and dug their way out of the nest. Mason put a finger up to his lips for them to be quiet. Sarah doubted noise would have bothered the turtles but they all watched in silence as the rest of the turtles dug their way out of the nest.

Aunt Virginia reached a gentle hand toward Janine, "It's time to let him go Janine. He needs to find his way to the creek water to survive."

Janine was reluctant at first but squatted down to carefully place the turtle on the grass. The little turtle took off running, its legs moving faster than something that size would be expected to move. Sarah remembered her father telling her that baby turtles ran to water to keep from being eaten by hawks and other predators.

Aunt Virginia, always mindful that Janine could not see what was going on around her, narrated to Janine how the turtle raced down the grassy yard, around the rocks that littered the creek banks, and into the water. It disappeared quickly into the current with its siblings. Janine jumped up and down clapping her hands together.

Rain began falling again so they took Janine back to the shelter of the porch. Aunt Virginia stopped on the porch to look over the railing at the wide green yard.

"Sometimes I get so caught up in fixing meals for the restaurant I forget to leave the kitchen and look at the world around me. I'm glad we heard Janine's giggles."

"Me too."

"Sarah, as you grow up, take the time to enjoy the little moments in life. God provides those moments to remind us there is more to life than our problems."

Sarah quietly thought about what her aunt said. She had never thought about God being interested in the small details of life.

John came after dark to take Sarah home. The darkness around them felt close and intimidating, the lantern he held not casting enough light. John held Sarah's hand. She walked close to him jumping at every sound in the woods surrounding them. Finally the corral near the house came into sight.

Once in the yard he handed Sarah the lantern. "Take the lantern inside, I'll check on Duke."

He knew his way to the barn without a light. Inside he lit a lantern, which was hanging next to Duke's stall. Duke greeted him with a whinny. John noticed the drawings hanging in the corner of the barn. He smiled at the faint smell that floated off the pictures as he walked closer to them.

His daughter's drawings of nature were amazing. His breath drew in when he saw the drawing of Mary. With his fingers he traced along the pencil lines of Mary's wavy hair flying in the breeze. Sarah had perfectly captured the look Mary would get on occasion when she was thinking about something. It made him remember the times they spent together in the early days of their marriage, picnicking in a field or walking the quiet streets of Williamsport in the cool evening temperatures.

He remembered asking her once, "What are you thinking about, Mary?"

She had looked sideways at him with a smile, paused in her task of trimming a rose stem from a shrub, "I'm dreaming about growing old with you John."

Another whinny from Duke brought John back to reality. Duke impatiently stretched his neck over the wall of his stall. John took a brush from a hook on the wall. He brushed Duke's coat and thought about better days with his wife. He looked at the pictures again, visible over the wall of the stall.

He also thought about what his sister had said to him that day. Virginia told him he was working too many hours, that Sarah needed quality time with her father. He remembered hearing the same words from his wife before things fell apart in their relationship. He knew he had to change in order to have better days with his daughter.

CHAPTER 11

Screams in the Night

That night, Sarah again dreamt again about Reverend Claythorn's retreating wagon. She was standing in the rain with her father, watching the wagon slowly disappear down the dirt road away from the church. Her mother was seated next to Reverend Claythorn in the wagon. He leaned in to whisper into her mother's ear. Her mother responded with a strong gaze toward Reverend Claythorn. Sarah screamed out in her sleep when Reverend Claythorn reached toward her mother's neck to choke her.

She woke up in the middle of a scream, sitting up in bed. And then a scream from outside startled her. Someone else was screaming near the cabin. She jumped out of bed terrified at what might be happening outside. When she ran into the kitchen she bumped into her father who was already in the living area in his pants and suspenders. He was reaching for the Winchester lever-action shotgun hanging above the front door.

"I'm scared!" Sarah grabbed him around the waist. Another scream made Sarah jump. Duke was kicking and loudly protesting from the barn.

"Stay inside." Her father commanded.

Sarah sat in the rocking chair near the fireplace. It was dark inside except for the moonlight shining through the window.

He paused one more time before opening the front door. "No matter what you hear, stay inside."

Sarah was pulling a blanket around her shaking shoulders.

"Sarah, do you understand?" He waited for her to answer.

"I will stay." She wrapped herself tightly in the blanket as if it would keep her safe from whatever was outside.

John cautiously stepped outside into the light of a full moon. He headed to the barn, looking around him each step he took. Just as he reached the barn door another scream came from the direction of the river. He jumped.

He checked to make sure the latch on the barn was secure. Leaning his back against the door he looked left and right for any movement. He looked at the field toward the creek but a cloud passing in front of the moon made it temporarily dark. When the moon cleared the clouds, he carefully scanned the field again. The moonlight pierced clearly through the trees on the far edge of the field, silhouetting the branches black against the sky.

A scream brought his attention to a treetop where he could see the silhouette of a large creature crouching on one of the branches. Although he had never seen one in person before, he was positive the dark outline was that of a panther. He followed his first instinct and ran back to the house.

When he entered the house Sarah was taking a hot kettle from the stove. "Did you see anything?"

John put the gun on the shelf but did not remove the ammunition like he usually did. "A panther."

Sarah was visibly frightened at the news. "Are we safe in here? What about Duke in the barn?"

John did not want to alarm his daughter more than was necessary. He tried to reassure her with his answer. "We are safe in the house. I made sure the barn door was secure. The panther is likely calling to a mate or hunting some deer."

"Would he go after something as large as Duke?"

"He looked very big. They usually go after easier prey, but I've heard stories that are difficult to believe."

Sarah was obviously still thinking about the cries they had heard. "It sounded like a woman being murdered!"

He answered calmly, "Many people have described the cry of a panther like that of a woman being murdered. I always thought it was an exaggeration until now."

Another scream came from further away. John sighed with relief. "I'm glad to hear it moving farther away from the house."

It was then John felt it safe to remove the ammunition from the gun, placing it over the door again. "Sarah, don't walk at dusk or in the dark alone. If you are in the woods, don't go without the bell I gave you. Did you see that newspaper article in Williamsport about the man who was dragged off by a panther?"

Sarah nodded her head.

He continued, "You don't want to surprise an animal like that."

Sarah stayed in the rocking chair. "I'm too scared to go back to bed, Father."

John had an idea. "I'll bring our mattresses out here. We can sleep by the fireplace tonight."

After adding wood to the fire, John brought the beds out. It took some time for the screams of the panther to leave their thoughts. They listened to the sound of the crackling fire. Sarah lay facing the fire, her head resting on her folded arms. "Father, why do you think Mother left us?"

It was quiet for a minute.

"A lot of things happened Sarah. I'm still figuring it out myself—we were happy for a long time, then—"

"Then what?"

"—Your Uncle Jacob and I were starting to do very well at the lumber business. We were making a lot of money in a short amount of time. The bank asked me to consider being on the board of directors, and then I was asked to be a deacon at the church. I forgot who the important people were in my life." He stoked the fire again with the fire iron. "I was working all the time, Sarah. Your mother tried to tell me."

He thought again about the talk his sister had with him about working too much. She told him that Sarah would soon be grown and he risked missing out on being a part of these years.

"Your mother asked me to stay home more. Eventually she stopped asking—I thought she had gotten used to everything. I was so busy I didn't notice things had changed between us."

John stared at the fire. He thought Mary would always be with him. He looked down at Sarah's face in the light of the fireplace. She looked so much like Mary.

Leia

"*Mother*" *by Sarah Richardson*

CHAPTER 12

Hog Butchering Day

Leia woke up before dawn to the sound of her mother gathering things from the kitchen. She remembered today was hog butchering day at Jeremiah and Ruby Mosley's barn. When she came into the kitchen, her mother was putting pies into a basket.

"Leia, can you get the ladle hanging over the stove?"

Her mother put the ladle in another basket filled with kitchen tools. Leia carried the basket, and they headed outside. Everything was frosty white in the cold morning air. The grass crackled under their feet as they walked toward the bridge.

Leia could see ice collecting around large rocks that rose up from the shallow creek bed. "Mother, I've never been to a hog butchering. How will I know what to do?"

"You can help me and the other ladies cook up a big breakfast, then we'll see where help is needed. You'll do fine."

On the other side of the stream they headed down a narrow road into a little hollow along a run that flowed into Lycoming Creek. When they reached the Mosley's red weathered barn, a number of people were already gathered in front around several large iron kettles. Double doors were open on both ends of the barn so one could see straight through the structure. Lanterns hung from the middle beam that ran the length of the building. Outside, three large kettles were already boiling. Leia glanced at the contents, curious what was cooking.

Her mother answered for her. "Those are hogs' heads boiling for scrapple. After it boils for a while, we will add cornmeal and spices to make the scrapple."

Leia crinkled her nose, "I never knew before what was in scrapple."

Her mother seemed amused with her reaction.

Pancakes, eggs, and sausages were being cooked over a low fire at the far side of the barn. Leia and her mother helped cook the sausages, turning them until they were golden brown before stacking them on a large platter. About eighteen people from town came to help with the butchering.

When breakfast was cleaned up, Leia was unsure what to do, so she followed her mother to the kettles.

A voice called to them from behind, "Caroline!"

Her mother turned in the direction of the familiar voice. "Ruby, how are you?"

When Leia turned she saw a tall beautiful black woman coming toward her mother who embraced Ruby then introduced Leia.

"Leia, I must introduce you to Jeremiah's wife, Ruby Mosely."

Leia offered her hand for a shake but Ruby quickly grabbed her into a hug. "No simple handshake for Caroline's daughter. I am so happy to finally meet you."

Leia had never seen hair like Ruby's. Beautiful braids covered her scalp with tiny colorful beads at the bottom of each. Her skin was a golden dark tone. High cheekbones and a large smile were the predominant features of her face.

Ruby spoke first, "If you don't mind, Caroline, I would like to take Leia with me. I will show her how to prepare the sausage skins."

Ruby took Leia to a long table full of pig intestines, which needed to be scraped and prepared for sausage. Ruby's hands were fast. She patiently stopped several times to help Leia improve her technique. By the second hour, Leia was scraping the skins almost as quickly. Leia was curious about Ruby but not bold enough to ask questions until after lunch. They were now seasoning sausage meat in large kettles, with handfuls of salt, pepper, and brown sugar.

Leia took a handful of salt from a barrel when she noticed a single snowflake land on her arm. She looked up to watch the first flakes of the season begin their journey to the ground. "I love watching the first snow of the season."

Ruby looked up at the grey sky. "I never saw snow until I was much older. I too have not lost the excitement over seeing the first snow."

Leia dropped her gaze to the sausage again, "I noticed your accent, where are you from originally?"

Ruby smiled as her skillful hands continued to work. "I was born in Africa, but when I was five my family was put on a slave ship headed for America. The accent you hear was picked up in Louisiana where I lived when I was older."

They continued sprinkling spices on the meat. Leia took a large flat ladle to fold and stir the meat in the kettles. Ruby worked on one next to hers.

Leia was curious to know Ruby's story. "Did you meet Jeremiah on the plantation?"

Ruby laughed. "I didn't meet him in the way you may think. Seven years after arriving in America, I was sold to a Louisiana slave owner to be given to a slave named Jeremiah. The owners wanted to breed future slaves."

Leia's ladle paused. It was difficult for her to fathom what Ruby had been through.

Ruby continued as she folded the meat. "Fortunately for me, Jeremiah was a good man. I didn't know it at the time, but he had the dream of being free."

"How did you come here?"

Ruby seemed comfortable sharing her story. "You ever hear the name Daniel Hughes?"

As a child, Leia had been fascinated with the history of the Underground Railroad and had come to know about a local figure named Daniel Hughes. "I do know that name. I tried to visit his grave in the Freedom Road Cemetery in Williamsport, but I was unable to find it because it was unmarked."

Ruby worked another handful of brown sugar into the meat. "It took six months for Jeremiah and me to make it all the way north to Canada, where we would be safe. I was pregnant with my oldest son, Jebediah, so the journey was slow. We didn't want our child born into slavery. Daniel Hughes helped us through Pennsylvania, hiding us in a house he had built from shrubs, feeding us, until it was safe to move on in the cover of darkness. When the war was over, we remembered this area and returned here to farm and raise our family."

A little black girl, who looked to be about five years old, interrupted the conversation carrying a very pregnant cat. "Mother, Mrs. Butler said I needed to ask you for permission to have candy. May I please?"

Ruby reached over to pet the black and white cat on the head and smiled at her daughter. "Yes, Jasmine you may have candy, but darling you need to let that cat walk on her own sometimes."

"But mother, she gets tired from carrying her babies around."

"Jasmine, say hello to Mrs. Richardson. She is Mrs. Oakley's daughter."

Jasmine put the cat down and reached a little hand toward Leia. "Nice to meet you, Mrs. Richardson. You have very pretty hair. Can I braid it sometime?"

"Jasmine!"

Leia was amused by Jasmine's frankness. "I don't mind Ruby."

Leia stooped down to Jasmine's level and looked into her dark eyes. "I would love it if you braided my hair sometime."

Jasmine responded simply by smiling and then took off running toward Mrs. Butler to retrieve some candy.

Leia was surprised by Ruby's next question. "Leia, what brings you here without your family?"

Leia looked down at the wedding band still on her left hand. She hadn't thought to take it off. Red burned into her cheeks.

"I left my family. It's a long complicated story."

Ruby stopped stirring the meat. "Leia, may I tell you more of my story?"

Leia nodded yes.

"After the slave boat arrived in Florida, I was taken away from my family, sold on an auction block like cattle. The only memories I have of my mother are the tight rows of braids in her hair. I can't remember the color of her eyes or what her face looked like; when I look into a mirror, I imagine that she had my color of eyes. All I can recall of my father is how he would sing in a deep voice when I was falling asleep at night on the ship.

I was beaten often by my owners and told I was no good. Every thought and feeling inside of me was consumed with growing hatred. When I was given to Jeremiah, he told me about a God who loved me. I thought it was a silly fantasy of his. It took years before I began to believe I was loved. Jeremiah was a good and patient man. There are times even now I feel so angry at what happened, at what I lost, but at some point I realized the hate I was holding inside had no effect on the people who took those things away from me. The hate was affecting my life."

Leia watched the changing emotions in Ruby's face as she told her story. She thought of her father and her own losses.

Ruby looked at Leia. "Leia, Caroline told me about your father. It must seem right to hate him, but it will rob you of the ability to really live life. The hate will convince you that your family deserves someone better, that you cannot be the mother and the wife you need to be."

Leia was surprised at Ruby's insight. "But—I don't think they could love me now after the things I have done."

"God still loves you, Leia. Your worth is not based on what your father said or what you have done, but by how much God loves you."

"My mother told me the same thing recently. I don't understand that kind of love."

Ruby smiled. "You could have run anywhere Leia, but God brought you here. You will understand God's love soon—of that I am very sure."

Leia worked silently next to Ruby. She noticed the snow collecting on the tree branches. It was beautiful. Leia looked up occasionally to watch her mother working on the other side of the barn with some other women. Her mother seemed happy here in spite of many years with an abusive husband.

When everything was cleaned up, the pork was divided among everyone. Leia walked home with her mother in silence, watching the snow thicken on the ground.

CHAPTER 13

The Common Hours

The first heavy snow came the same day the train arrived with the supplies ordered from the list Sarah and her aunt made. Even though the train came every day, the train station was full of people who came to watch it arrive. The small crowd reminded Sarah of the days in Williamsport when she and Kassie would watch the packer boats on the Susquehanna River. Mr. Wagner, a single man who owned the general store, stood off to the side waiting for deliveries for his store. The only woman in the crowd was Mrs. Jensen from the boarding house. Sarah noticed a bruise on Mrs. Jensen's chin, but quickly forgot about it when a whistle sounded and a pillar of smoke appeared around the bend of the tracks.

The ground shook as the great iron train slowed to a stop in front of the station. Everyone moved forward as the loading ramps were lowered from the boxcars, and then it was orderly chaos as men helped unload the goods, making stacks of items on the wide wooden platform in front of the station. Mr. Milton took a large bag containing the mail, which he carried to the post office. One of the boxcars contained various kinds of livestock. Sarah was surprised when her father placed a crate of chickens at her feet. Inside the crate were a beautiful tom and chicken, agitated at their confinement, clucking their opinion loudly. Her father helped Mr. Wagner load supplies onto his wagon then walked to the post office. Sarah followed along with the clucking crate bouncing against her skirts with every step she took.

Mr. Milton had a letter for her from Kassie, and her father received some mail from Wellsboro. Their wagon was parked next to the general store. Sarah put the chicken crate in the back of the wagon covered it with a blanket to keep the chicks warm, and then she helped her father with the list of things they had ordered at the general store.

When everything was loaded into the wagon, they started home. Sarah put the letter from Kassie inside her coat pocket. She could hardly wait to get home and read it. She pushed her lace-up boots against the front of the wagon hoping Duke would trot a little faster. When she looked down at her shoes, she noticed her dress looked a little short and her coat was higher up on her arms than normal. She was getting taller and hadn't thought about adding clothes to the supply list. She pulled her gloves higher to cover the gap where cold air was blowing up her sleeve. If her mother were here, she would have made her something before Sarah even noticed she was outgrowing her things. She sighed. Large snowflakes started falling from grey clouds.

When they reached home, Sarah jumped down from the wagon ready to unload supplies, but her father stopped her as she unhooked the rope across the back of the wagon. "Why don't you go inside, get a fire going, and read your letter. I can unload these supplies myself, and take care of Duke."

She ran to the wood stack next to the front door, filling her arms with three logs before going inside. Her father opened the door for her before going to the barn.

She hollered out after him, "Thank you, Father!"

She ran inside, threw her scarf, hat, and gloves on the hooks next to the door in a hurry to get the fire started. As soon as the fire was reaching up from the kindling onto the bottom log, she pulled the rocker close to the fireplace, and opened the envelope.

Dear Sarah,

I miss you so much. It isn't the same here without you. I miss running along the riverbanks with you and baking bread with you and your mother.

After you left town, someone broke all of the windows in the church. A lot of people were very upset about Reverend Claythorn leaving so it could have been anyone. Thankfully, people are not talking much about Reverend Claythorn anymore.

Father says we need to go to church to learn about God. I thought that is why we were going in the first place, but he has been different since you and Uncle John left.

Wayne is up to his usual ways at school. Last week he put a frog in the teacher's desk drawer and she jumped on her desk and hollered until everyone was laughing hysterically. She was very angry. We were all sent home early, and Wayne isn't allowed back until after Christmas. Rumor is that he is going to work with his father on the farm and that he's not coming back to school at all.

The thought of your family not being here to sing carols and hang popcorn on the tree is unbearable! I wish things were back to the way they were before.

I hope you are doing well. I cannot imagine what it must be like to live in the wilderness. I read stories in the papers sometimes that make me wonder how you are faring. Give my greetings to Uncle John, Aunt Virginia, Uncle Harold, Mason, and Janine. Write soon.

I included an extra paper with this letter explaining where we are in our studies at school.

Love,
Kassie

Sarah missed Kassie. If her mother hadn't run away she would still be in Williamsport living in the house next to Kassie. Sarah ran to the barn where her drawings hung. She needed to see the picture she had drawn of her mother looking off into the distance, but the drawing wasn't there anymore. She scuffed the hay around on the floor of the barn under where the pictures hung, thinking it had fallen from the string. Her father was in the barn giving some oats to Duke. "Father, did you see any of my drawings on the floor when you were raking the hay?"

He looked over the edge of a stall. "Missing one?"

Sarah couldn't say she was looking for her mother's picture, because she didn't want to say the word "mother" right now. "I must have taken one inside. I'll look in my room," Sarah replied.

She left the barn to look in her drawing book by her bed, but it wasn't there either.

She paused to look at her room with the simple bed and nightstand. She was remembering her second-story bedroom in Williamsport, which overlooked the front yard gardens. Because of her parents, she had lost everything familiar in her life. After dinner, she sat at the table and drew another picture of her mother. This time Sarah drew tears running down her mother's face. When it was finished she took it to the barn to hang next to the other drawings.

Sarah and her father were invited to the hotel for Thanksgiving dinner. Sarah was feeling easily irritated. Mason and Janine quickly decided to play on their own when she snapped at them after they tried to crawl on her lap.

After dinner, her aunt asked her for help. "Sarah, help me carry the dishes into the kitchen so we can bring the apple pie out."

Sarah did as she was asked.

In the kitchen Aunt Virginia addressed her. "Sarah, how are you doing?"

"Fine." Sarah started to pump water into the sink for the dirty dishes.

Aunt Virginia was persistent. "It doesn't seem like you are doing fine to me. You are somewhere else in your thoughts. Do you realize you scared Mason and Janine when you snapped at them before dinner?"

"I'm sorry, Aunt Virginia. I didn't realize I had done that. I'm thinking a lot about home and my mother."

Aunt Virginia sympathized, "Sarah, this is your first Thanksgiving without your mother. I can imagine it is difficult for you and your father."

Sarah agreed. "Aunt Virginia, I love getting to know you all better. I'm glad we are having Thanksgiving dinner here, but—I think this whole thing with mother leaving and us moving here, is unfair. I miss my room; I really miss cousin Kassie with whom I have been since birth, and I miss my mother!"

Her Aunt reached in the pantry for caramel sauce.

Sarah didn't stop. "Aunt Virginia, did you know my mother left without saying goodbye or even saying 'I love you'? I keep wondering if she still loves me. Why would she leave if she still loved us?"

Sarah was close to tears. Aunt Virginia reached her arms around Sarah. "I'm sorry you are so sad, Sarah." Her aunt was quiet for a moment then spoke again. "I just had a memory come to me."

Sarah looked up at her aunt waiting.

"You probably don't realize I was there when you were born."

Sarah wondered why her aunt was bringing up her birth. "I didn't know you were around when I was born."

"I hadn't met Uncle Harold yet, and I was living with Jacob and Katherine for a little while. Your mother was very sick during her pregnancy. She needed the extra help around the house." Aunt Virginia was drizzling caramel on the apple slices as she talked. "Your grandmother passed away three months before you were born. Mary took the loss of her mother very hard—then you were born." She put the jar of caramel on the counter and looked at Sarah. "When you were born, it was suddenly as if everything was right again with her. She was so happy when she took you in her arms for the first time. She loved you very much, but Sarah no matter how much your mother tried to cover it up, there was something sad inside her. Sometimes, if I caught her alone in the garden or doing housework, I would see a faraway look, like she was hiding a hurt she had never shared with anyone. Something troubled her deeply. I wish now that I had asked her about it."

"Why didn't you, Aunt Virginia?"

"Because I met Uncle Harold and became caught up in my own love story."

Aunt Virginia's eyes reflected the pain that she felt for her. "Sarah, you will need to forgive your mother."

This is not the message Sarah expected to hear. "But Aunt Virginia, she left us."

"You can't change the fact that she left you, but if you do not forgive her, you will lose the ability to experience joy in your life."

Sarah was hoping for more sympathy. "How can I be happy with the knowledge she left me? I have lost so many things because of her choices."

"Only you can decide to be happy, Sarah. Yes, you will grieve and you will hurt because you love your mother, but don't let it turn your heart bitter. Don't let the wrongs in your life overshadow all the good things that happen." She quietly listened to her aunt. "Sarah, when you walk in the woods, or when Mason runs up to you and shouts out that you're pretty, or when you get sprayed with a skunk but rescued by Matthew, or you see hatching turtles run to water, those are the often forgotten common hours in which we live. When you learn to be grateful for those little moments, you will learn to enjoy life no matter what it brings."

"But Aunt Virginia, it seems impossible to see things that way."

"Sarah, start one little moment at a time. You can begin with enjoying some pie in the company of your family."

Her aunt carried two plates through the kitchen door. Sarah stayed in the kitchen for a few moments thinking about what her Aunt had just said. She sat in a short chair at Mason and Janine's table. Her eyes were drawn to an etching in the tabletop. A small heart with an arrow through it was next to the word Sarah. She smiled. Her nephew had such a big heart. She rubbed her fingers along the rough edge of the etching thinking about the times she had been able to spend with her cousins since coming to Slate Run. She looked at the two plates of pie on the counter. It was time to act on Aunt Virginia's advice to start one moment at a time enjoying the common hours. She stood up from the chair, took the two plates of pie from the counter, and walked through the door to the dining room to join her family.

It was dusk by the time Sarah and her father left for home. She was glad that in spite of everything she had Aunt Virginia to help her. She noticed how the snow floated in the air, and the cold wind blew the bare tree branches. Snow collected in the grooves of the frozen ground. She noticed Duke was oddly stomping his hooves. "Father, what is Duke doing? Do you think he minds the snow?"

A flash of dark fur in the shrubs to the left of the wagon caught her attention. They were being followed.

Her father noticed too. "Settle down Duke." He spoke calmly, but Sarah could hear the nervousness in his voice.

"Did you see it father?"

He whispered, "Yes, I think it's the panther."

Sarah sat up, searching the dusky landscape. She held tightly on to her father's arm. All she could think about was being dragged into the woods by a panther like the man in the newspaper article.

She clung even tighter when she saw the panther a few yards away. Duke stepped a little quicker toward home. When they passed an area of thick shrubs she lost sight of the creature. Not knowing where the panther was made her even more nervous. When they arrived home, her father secured Duke in the barn. Although she felt safer inside, she was unsettled because of the panther. Sarah realized how thankful she was she still had her father and her family in Slate Run. That night she prayed she would never get dragged away by a panther.

CHAPTER 14

A Day With Father

By December the ground was covered in a heavy blanket of snow. The air was cold, but the sky was cloudless. The snow sparkled off of the field like diamonds. Because it was too cold and icy for Sarah to be hiking the mountain, she spent a lot of time in the kitchen with Aunt Virginia. Sometimes she would look at the smoke curling up from the Stephens' ranch on the mountaintop and wonder what Matthew was doing or when she might see him again. She missed being around people her age, most of all Kassie. Today she was helping her aunt make apple pies. The smell of the rich sugary sauce cooking with the soft apples was comforting against the cold air outside. When the pies were done, Aunt Virginia gave her some money. Sarah thought she was sending her to the general store for supplies.

"Sarah, you have been a tremendous help in the restaurant. Christmas is coming up, and I thought you might like to have some money to get your father something."

Sarah looked at the coins in her hand. She never had her own money before. She smiled at her aunt. "But Aunt Virginia, you don't have to pay me; I'm your niece!"

"Just because you are my niece doesn't mean you work for free. You have been a huge help. I don't know what I would have done without your help during this pregnancy."

"Thank you, I'll be able to get something nice for father, and I've never been able to do that before. I feel so grown up!"

When she finished helping with lunch Sarah walked to the general store to find a gift for her father. She looked at the barrels of pickles, shelves of stock feed, and food supplies stacked in rows at the back of the store. She looked at wooden barrels filled with interesting items like spyglasses, pocket knives, shoe polish, and other practical items. She overheard some gentlemen talking to Mr. Wagner who were in the store picking up supplies.

"I saw the panther too. It killed one of my chickens!"

"Panthers don't usually come after people, but it's unsettling when they come so close to the house."

After Mr. Wagner finished their order he noticed Sarah looking at the items in the barrels. "Sarah, can I help you find something?"

"Well—" She put down a red pocket knife she was considering as a gift. "I would like to get a Christmas gift for my father. Do you have any suggestions Mr. Wagner?"

He thought for a moment. "What about a flannel shirt?"

Sarah wasn't sure.

Mr. Wagner showed her all of the gadgets she had just looked at in the buckets but nothing seemed to be the perfect gift. Suddenly Mr. Wagner walked to a shelf behind the cash register. "I know just the thing!" He seemed very excited. "Why didn't I think of this right away?" He pulled a book from the shelf and handed it to Sarah.

She looked at the leather-bound cover.

Thirty Years a Hunter
Philip Tome

"I received these new copies in my last delivery. Mr. Tome and his family were the first white people to settle in this area. This book is full of hunting stories from his time in the valley. I saw your father looking at it the last time he was in here."

Sarah agreed it would be a good gift. She gave Mr. Wagner twenty cents for the book, and he wrapped it in brown paper and twine for her. She was so happy with her find that she ran home. She would keep it safe under her mattress until Christmas Eve.

Father's Winchester lever-action shotgun was always hanging above the front door. Sarah knew she was never to touch it. One sunny cold morning, her father surprised her by staying home from work. He told her to dress warmly because after breakfast he was going to teach her how to use the shotgun.

"There may be a time when you are here alone and a panther or something else comes around. You should know how to safely use the gun."

Sarah was excited at the prospect of learning to use a gun. They walked out into the field by the house where he had already set up a crate with a plank of wood on top to act as the target.

"Sarah, before you even touch a gun, you need to know how to handle one safely. Never point a gun at a person, even if you think there is no ammunition in the gun. Even when I'm cleaning a gun, I make sure the barrel is pointed away from people." He told her other things like making sure of the target before firing, and unloading the gun when it was not in use. After a lesson on safety he was ready to show her how to use the shotgun.

Her father pulled a lever downward and the barrel appeared to break away from the gun. He looked down the barrel, loaded some shots then closed the barrel again. He handed her the gun.

"Tuck it tightly into your shoulder, like this."

He demonstrated first, showing her how to fit the gun between her arm and shoulder muscles.

She did exactly as she was shown.

He continued to instruct her how to focus on the target using the sights on the barrel.

"Now look down the barrel with one eye. The metal pieces sticking up from the barrel are called sights. Concentrate on them with one eye, especially the front sight. The target should be slightly out of focus. Use your rear sight to center the front sight. The tops of the sights should be level."

"When you are ready, gently, not quickly, squeeze the trigger."

He stepped away to give her room.

She squeezed the trigger. The gun recoiled hard against her arm, the barrel bouncing up into the air as a loud bang exploded from the end of the barrel.

"Wow!" Sarah could feel adrenaline rushing through her veins. She massaged her shoulder and held the gun to her side with her right arm.

"Try again, Sarah. It looks like you hit near the bottom left of the board. Make sure you hold the gun high enough. Fire when you're ready."

This time her father had her break the barrel, load the ammunition and pull the hammer back. She put the gun tight into her shoulder, eyed the sights, and gently squeezed the trigger.

"Boom!" The gun slammed against her shoulder again and it rose up slightly. This time the board went flying off the wooden crate.

"Yeah!" Sarah couldn't help screaming out her excitement.

Her father took the gun and walked across the field with her to inspect the target, which was lying behind the crate. He held it up to her and smiled. The top third of the board was blown away.

"Good job, Sarah!" He put the board on the crate again. She fired a number of rounds until her arms were shaking from the weight of the gun and her shoulder ached from the recoil.

"That's enough for today, Sarah; let's have some lunch."

They ate sandwiches and leftover apple pie.

Her father had another announcement after lunch. "I have a surprise for you Sarah."

She finished putting away their plates on the shelf above the sink. "What is it, Father?"

"Today we are going to find our Christmas tree."

Sarah put the linen towel down used to dry the dishes and ran to her room, "I'll be ready in one minute!"

He looked happy at her enthusiasm. "We'll walk Duke with us. He can pull the tree home for us. Meet me by the barn."

Her father put an axe and the shotgun in the saddle before they headed into the forest. The way was steep until they reached a high meadow of hemlock trees. They surprised a flock of turkey that was quick to notice the intruders and fluttered into the shelter of nearby shrubs. Sarah saw the tree she wanted on the far side of the meadow. It was perfectly shaped and very tall.

Her father voiced concern over her choice. "I think this will touch the ceiling in our cabin. Are you sure this is the one Sarah?"

Sarah was determined. "I think it's perfect!"

After chopping down the tree he tied it to the back of the saddle so it would drag behind Duke as they made their way home.

"I wonder what mother will be doing for Christmas?" Sarah spoke out loud then wished she had kept it to herself. She didn't want to spoil the perfect day they were having.

Her father didn't answer.

They reached Pine Creek at the place where it flowed through the splash dam. In winter a gate in the middle of the dam was left open to allow water to flow through. Her father stopped on the creek bank looking south. A large elk was crossing the creek about a hundred yards downstream. The massive size of the elk took Sarah by surprise. Duke impatiently shook his bridle, which spooked the elk back into the woods.

When they reached home, her father pulled the tree inside and put it into a bucket Sarah had placed across the room from the fireplace. As soon as he put the tree upright, it bent forward under the ceiling, almost toppling down onto him. The tree was about a foot too tall.

Sarah laughed while she tried to help her father hold the tree. "Oops, I guess I was thinking about our ceiling at the house in Williamsport. I should have listened to you."

His arms were wrapped around the tree, deep inside the branches. He bent backwards to stick his head out of the branches. She could see he was laughing.

He struggled with the tree before he was able to pull it down to the floor. "I think we will have to trim the top."

"Sorry, father, I'll get the ax from the barn."

That evening after finishing the tree, they sat by the fire sipping hot tea. They were pleased with their work, even if the tree did stop abruptly before resting against the ceiling. When she finished her tea, Sarah reached into her yarn basket for her math book.

Her father had been whittling away on a piece of wood for a while when he looked up from his work, "I also wonder what Mary is doing for Christmas and where she is."

Sarah had forgotten about the question she had asked earlier. She kept all of her mixed feelings inside of her but realized her father was dealing with a lot of emotions too.

CHAPTER 15

Winter and Difficult Times

Fresh snow had fallen overnight, which would make tracking turkeys easier. Uncle Harold and her father were gone before sunup hoping to get Sunday dinner before the day was over. When there was enough light in the sky, Sarah walked to the hotel to help her aunt in the kitchen. Aunt Virginia's stomach was getting really big, which made it more difficult for her aunt to get around. Sarah wondered if she would have the baby before March.

Sarah removed a cloth from a large crock to pull out some raised bread dough. She started punching and rolling the dough on the large wood-topped island in the middle of the kitchen.

Her aunt was watching her. "Sarah, you actually look like you know what you're doing."

Sarah continued to fold and punch the dough with a feeling of contentment. Her aunt went into the pantry to retrieve some canned meat for stew. They worked through the lunch hour. A number of new men had arrived in town to work on peeling hemlock bark for the tanneries.

Mason and Janine were taking afternoon naps when the church bell began to ring. Aunt Virginia came out of the pantry with a jar in her hand. "Something's happened!"

Sarah wiped her floured hands on her apron. "I'll run to the church to find out."

Her aunt said nothing but gave her approval with the nod of her head. When Sarah ran out the door, Aunt Virginia was still standing near the pantry with the jar in her hands.

Sarah raced to the church. With every step she ran she had one thought in her mind: *Please, God, don't let anything happen to father, please.*

By midday Harold had gotten a turkey. They decided to stay out longer in spite of the near zero temperature, so John could also get a turkey. By the time they reached a high mountain meadow, the sun was glaring from its highest point in the sky off the white snow. The only sighting of a turkey since Harold had gotten his had been two toms that were obscured by low-lying brush and too far away. Harold had to convince John they should stop to eat something before continuing to hunt. He shared some venison jerky Virginia had made. Sarah had packed enough bread and fried chicken for her father and uncle to share.

Harold sat down with some beef jerky in his hand. "What do you think of country life, John?"

"I like how quiet it is here when the mill isn't running, and all the wildlife." He smiled at the irony of his statement, "Although the wildlife seems scarce at the moment."

Harold agreed. "I love the quiet here too. It will be interesting to see how things change when everything has been lumbered from the mountains."

John wasn't sure if his brother-in-law was giving him a personal message against the lumber industry. He remembered his sister had expressed mixed feelings when the lumber boom had begun. In Williamsport, the general consensus was in favor of the industry that was making many of them millionaires. He could understand people who lived in the country having different feelings as they watched the beauty of their surroundings and the wildlife they hunted disappear from the thinning woods. When clearcutting the wilderness had begun a few years ago, the newspapers had been filled with the voices of opposition. Sometimes John felt conflicted, but he didn't know what else he could do that would provide such a good living for his family.

Harold interrupted his thoughts again. "That daughter of yours has been a big help to Virginia."

John was proud of the young lady his daughter had become. "It has been good for her to be with Virginia. Even as a child, Virginia was the nurturing sister to Jacob and me. She was always the one that took care of us when we were sick or injured."

Harold smiled. "That sounds like my Virginia. The way she watches over Janine and makes sure she sees everything we experience through words amazes me."

They paused, eating the chicken and bread.

"Harold, I didn't know how we would make it without Mary. Virginia has provided what Sarah needs right now emotionally."

Harold finished his drumstick. "Will you return to Williamsport next year?"

John hadn't given much thought to his future plans. "I honestly don't know. Jacob and Katherine are in town, but I'm not ready to go back to our home where we were a family for so many years."

Harold put extra lunch items in his saddlebag. "Will you try to find Mary?"

John had asked himself this question many times. "I think she will come back when she is ready."

John was tired from the conversation, his mind filling with memories from the past year. He put his water leather back into his saddle. "It's time we go back to finding that turkey before it gets dark."

Another hour passed without sight of any turkey. John finally resolved to the reality that he would not be getting one today. "We might as well head down the mountain."

"Sorry John, maybe next week."

John, although disappointed, was inwardly glad to be heading home to a warm fire.

They started the steep descent down the mountain, John feeling tired and discouraged. He wasn't paying attention to the trail when a branch caught him across the face. He reached up to hold the branch away from him just as Duke slipped on a patch of ice hidden by snow. Duke jerked suddenly to the left, and John with only one hand on the bridle, slipped part way off the saddle to the right. He grabbed the bridle with both hands, trying to pull himself back up. The ravine, next to the path, dove steeply below him to the run where water flowed under a thin sheet of ice. The snow under Duke's hooves hid more ice. The weight of John hanging off the side pulled the horse closer to the edge. Not able to get his grip, John fell off the saddle, sliding down the steep snowy ravine. Duke pulled down by the force of John sliding off was crashing toward him.

Having heard the commotion Harold turned back and rushed to the side of the ravine in time to see John splashing into the icy run. Duke landed on the snowy bank above the run. Harold shouted down to John but John remained in the water apparently unconscious. The only relief Harold had was that the water was too shallow to flow over John's head. Finding a rope in his saddlebag, he quickly tied it around a tree and lowered himself part way down the hill. At the end of the rope he scrambled past Duke who was standing up but obviously favoring his right front leg. Duke was tossing his head and protesting until Harold reached John.

Harold anchored his boots against a large rock to pull John's body out of the freezing water. Knowing he had to act fast, he stripped John's coat, shirt and gloves from him, replacing them with his own shirt, coat, and gloves. He placed his hat under John's head before rubbing the skin on Johns face to bring some warmth to the surface. Harold looked around him at the ravine, calculating a way up without Duke, who was limping on one of his legs. Knowing he had no choice but to leave John in the ravine, he quickly scrambled back up the hill to his own horse. He raced to town his chest and arms fully exposed to the biting cold air.

When Sarah reached the church, she saw her uncle shirtless, ringing the bell. Mr. Milton from the post office reached the church first, closely followed by some woodhicks who were staying at the boarding house. Mr. Milton gave her uncle a coat. The men were already planning a rescue when Sarah reached him.

She grabbed her uncle's hand to get his attention. "Uncle Harold, what's going on?"

"Sarah, your father fell into a ravine." He stepped close to her, bending down slightly. The other men talked with each other, some of them riding away presumably to gather supplies. "Listen carefully Sarah, I need you to run to the hotel to ask Aunt Virginia for a shirt, coat, gloves and hat."

"But Uncle Harold—"

"Quickly, Sarah."

Her uncle turned to the men. Sarah ran to the restaurant. Her aunt had been watching for her because the door to the kitchen opened as soon as she reached it.

"Aunt Virginia! There has been an accident. Uncle Harold needs a shirt, hat, and gloves." Her aunt wasted no time gathering the items, with the addition of a blanket. She gave them to Sarah with quick instructions.

"Find out what you can, Sarah."

When Sarah returned to the church the men were on horses. Her uncle returned the loaned coat to Mr. Milton as he put on the fresh clothes. He took the blanket. "Good idea, Sarah."

He mounted his horse, and before Sarah could ask anything the men were headed up the mountain.

It was dusk when she rushed back to the hotel. Her aunt looked anxious to hear news. "Well?"

"Aunt Virginia, there was no time to ask questions. All I know is that Father has fallen into a ravine."

Sarah, breathless from running, couldn't say anything more.

Her aunt looked around the kitchen. "We need to be ready when the men return. They will need hot stew and coffee to warm themselves up." She took a large pan from above the stove. "Sarah, I need you to make the bed in the guestroom upstairs. Your father may need to stay here if he is injured or sick from the cold."

Sarah's pulse was racing her thoughts overwhelming her. "Aunt Virginia, I can't lose father too—"

"I know, honey—" Her aunt hugged her holding Sarah's head against her chest.

"Let's pray for your father and all the men headed toward him right now."

Mason and Janine were playing in the parlor unaware of what was going on. Sarah could hear them giggling.

Aunt Virginia motioned her to the breakfast table to pray with her. Sarah found her aunt's words comforting as she prayed for her brother, John, and the men who were going to help. She even prayed for Duke which made Sarah's mind jump.

Duke! She hadn't thought about Duke.

When her aunt said "amen" they both hurried to their tasks.

Sarah finished preparing the bed upstairs then helped in the kitchen. It was good to have something to keep her busy while they waited. Sarah could see her aunt's lips moving silently as she continued praying. Sarah was grateful for the prayers.

Noise at the side porch announced the arrival of the men. Sarah ran outside, immediately noticing the makeshift bed that had been pulled behind Mr. Milton's horse. She ran to her father's side. He was unconscious. She looked at her aunt hoping she would say something to stop the panic she felt at the sight of her father.

Her aunt appeared just as alarmed. She reached a hand to his forehead then raised her head looking for Harold who was standing behind her, "Harold, I need Alice here!"

Her uncle didn't even hesitate as he mounted his horse taking off toward the bridge.

Three young woodhicks, who had helped in the rescue, stepped forward and asked how they could help. Sarah heard her aunt telling them where the guest room was upstairs and asked them to carry him there.

Sarah noticed Duke when she stepped aside for them to carry her father. Duke was standing behind the group. Mr. Milton was examining his leg. She ran to Duke who greeted her with a shake of his head and a whinny. She hugged his nose.

"Mr. Milton, will Duke be okay?"

"His leg joint is swollen some, but he is a strong horse. I'll wrap his leg tight to support the muscles then I'll put him in your uncle's barn for the night."

Mr. Milton massaged Duke's leg again. "With rest he should be fine, Sarah. You go inside to help with your father. He will want to see you when he wakes up."

Sarah ran upstairs; the three men who had carried her father inside were standing awkwardly in the room, not sure what to do next.

Her aunt was throwing extra blankets over her brother. Finally noticing the men, she let them go, "Thank you for bringing John up; downstairs you will find hot stew and coffee on the stove. Sit by the fire and don't leave for home until you are completely warm. We don't need anyone else around here sick."

"Yes, ma'am." They left hurriedly, glad there was hot stew waiting for them.

Mrs. Alice Jensen showed up in the doorway of the room with a small black bag in her hand. "I'll take care of John, Virginia. You tend to Harold. He was exposed to the cold too long. Let me know if he shows any signs of fever."

Mrs. Jensen leaned down to touch John's forehead then held his wrist in her hand before she directed orders to Aunt Virginia who stood as if in shock by the rocking chair in the corner. "I can take care of this patient, Virginia. It's very important you take care of your husband. If you don't stop him, he will try to finish putting away the horses and the equipment."

Mrs. Jensen was already at work warming up father's legs and arms by rubbing her hands vigorously on his skin, when her aunt left the room.

"Sarah, get a bowl of warm water and rags from the kitchen."

For a while she was busy getting supplies and food. Then all she could do was wait in the rocking chair in the corner of her father's room, watching Mrs. Jensen. He slept. A bandage was wrapped around his head from forehead to hairline, covering the injury on his head. Sarah relaxed into the rocking chair, but she couldn't close her eyes, which never left her father's face. *Please, God, I can't lose him. Please, God…*

Despite her resolve to keep watch over her father, exhaustion finally took over. When she awoke in the early hours of morning, Mrs. Jensen was pouring water from a pitcher into a bowl.

"Good morning, Sarah. I'm glad you were able to sleep because your father is going to need your help today."

Sarah ran to her father's bed. He was still sleeping. She looked up at Mrs. Jensen. "Is he going to wake up?"

Mrs. Jensen cautiously reassured her. "He started running a fever overnight. When the fever breaks, he should wake up and recover just fine."

Mrs. Jensen started to gather things back into her black bag. "Sarah, I will return this afternoon to check on your father. He has a small injury on his head. Leave the bandages on; I will change them tomorrow. The most important thing right now is to watch his temperature. Feel his forehead occasionally or notice if he is sweating. Keep a wet cloth on his head to draw the temperature down."

Mrs. Jensen left. In the hallway she heard her talking to her aunt. Sarah touched the cloth on her father's forehead that Mrs. Jensen had placed there. It was cool to her touch. When she put her hands on his face his skin burned against them. *If I lose father—* She sat in the chair next to his bed, holding his hand in hers.

Her aunt put a cot in the room for Sarah to sleep on for the two days that her father rested, unconscious with fever. The afternoon of the third day, his fever dropped. Sarah was resting her hand on his forehead when he opened his eyes. He wrapped his arms around her as she laid her head on his chest. They clung to each other, grateful to still be together.

With rest and good care from her aunt, her uncle had avoided fever. Four days after the accident, He took Sarah and her father home in his sled with Duke tethered to the back of the sled.

When they arrived at the cabin her uncle helped her father, who was still regaining his strength, inside. Before leaving, he set up a bed in the living area near the fireplace, started a fire, and made sure there was enough firewood inside the cabin for Sarah. Uncle Harold also took the time to show Sarah how to care for Duke's leg.

Thankfully, after a week of rest, her father was able to get from the house to the barn but was exhausted by the time he had fed the animals. He grumbled a lot about how much rest he needed. Sarah knew that it was hard for him to not be so independent.

Sarah and her father had a heightened awareness of how much they had almost lost. They talked often after dinner, by the fire.

"Father, I pray every night that mother will come back." Sarah looked right at him. "But it's been so long since she left that part of me believes I will never see her again."

Her father was pouring hot tea into a cup. "Sarah, there is something I have never told you before."

She had been crocheting a blanket in the dim light of the fireplace. Her needles paused in their work.

He came near the fire, leaning an arm on the mantle. "When your mother was pregnant with you, she disappeared for a little while."

"What do you mean disappeared? Aunt Virginia mentioned she was helping mother when she was pregnant with me. Did this happen while Aunt Virginia was there?"

"Yes, she was there when it happened."

"Why didn't she tell me?"

"Probably because none of us ever figured out where she went or why."

Her father added more wood to the fire. "When your grandfather Graham died the year before, she took it very hard. Then three months before you were born, your grandmother Lillian died. After the funeral, Mary became emotionally reclusive. None of us thought much about it, because we knew she was grieving her parents so much." He paused again, fidgeting with his hands. "One day while Aunt Virginia was out getting items at the general store, Mary disappeared. She left without leaving any word as to her whereabouts. We thought at first she must have taken a walk down by the river, but when nightfall came and she still hadn't returned, we knew something was wrong. Aunt Virginia, Uncle Jacob, Aunt Katherine, and I looked for her for three days."

Sarah was shocked at what she was hearing. "It took three days to find her?"

"We never found her. Three days after she disappeared she was home again, apologetic she had caused worry, but no explanation except she had needed to mourn in private. She did seem a little better, so we all chose to forget about it in spite of our misgivings."

Sarah and her father were quiet for a while, thinking about Mary.

"Father, Aunt Virginia said she thought mother might have had a secret. Did you ever think that about her?"

"There were times, especially early in our marriage, when I would swat at a fly or reach for something, Mary would flinch as if I was going to hit her. I have only seen someone do that who has been abused. It was difficult for me to imagine what could have happened in her past that would make her react in that way, especially because her parents Lillian and Graham were such gentle people. It seemed easier to not ask the difficult questions, but looking back I know that was wrong. I should not have let her fight her battles alone."

In the flickering light of the fire, they talked for hours about her mother and their life in Williamsport.

CHAPTER 16

Christmas Fire

The snow was so deep now that the shoveled path to the barn was lined on each side with waist-high snow. Whenever Sarah went outside she layered with a hat, a scarf around her ears and mouth, long mittens, two coats, two layers of wool socks, and boots. The snow underfoot was crunchy, frozen in the cold temperatures. Pine Creek was almost frozen from one bank to the other, flowing narrowly through a sliver in the middle where the water still moved too fast for freezing. Sarah could see water bubbles under the thin ice as the water under it flowed.

At night when Sarah wasn't studying her schoolbooks or crocheting, she was drawing pictures, most of them glimpses of the winter scenes. She drew a wagon wheel leaning against the barn, outlined in white snow, blades of dry wheat sticking up through the snow. Her sketches stayed in her drawing book in the crochet basket next to the fireplace.

On Christmas Eve day she baked an apple cobbler at the hotel for her father and her to enjoy after Christmas dinner. While her father was tending to Duke in the barn that evening, Sarah raced into her room to get his gift and placed it far under the tree branches. Later, they strung popcorn to decorate the tree and tied red ribbons on the branches. Her father played the harmonica and told stories. Sarah wished her mother were here with them. Sarah wondered where her mother was celebrating the holidays and if she was happy. Even though it was late when they went to bed, it was a long time before Sarah could go to sleep. She was excited about having a gift for her father.

Sarah woke up early, shivering in the cold room. She tiptoed out to the stove to warm her hands; it would soon need more wood. When her hands were warm enough, she turned around to warm her back. Something outside the kitchen window caught her eye. She stepped closer to the window. There were a number of turkeys in the field, pecking at the ground. A grey cloud rose above the trees in the direction of the bridge. She squinted into the early morning light. A flash of orange shot high through the cloud.

Without a thought she screamed, "Fire! Father, Fire!"

She pounded on her father's bedroom door.

He opened the door already in a pair of pants and suspenders. "I saw it too, Sarah!"

She was worried about where the fire was coming from. "It's by the bridge, Father; what if it's the hotel?"

He ran back into his room to retrieve his flannel shirt. "Sarah, get dressed as quickly as you can then walk in the direction of the fire. Bring extra pails for water!"

He pulled on his hat, coat, and boots, before running outside. He didn't take the time to hitch up the sleigh, running the distance to town. The church bell was ringing to call everyone to the fire.

Sarah did as her father said, bringing extra pails for water. She ran down the road slipping on icy patches here and there. When she reached the bridge she could see that the restaurant was not on fire, but the Jensen's boarding house was consumed in flames. When she reached Main Street, she noticed Mr. Milton outside in his long johns, pants, and overalls, throwing buckets of water on the post office, which was dangerously threatened by the growing fire. The church bell stopped ringing as most of the town's people had arrived. Everyone was carrying buckets.

A line quickly formed, from the water pump near the home on the far side of the boarding house all the way to the post office. One person pumped the water; another filled the bucket, another passed it along the line of people. Water was thrown on the boarding house and the post office.

Aunt Virginia was the one who realized Mr. Jensen was nowhere to be found. She rushed to Alice who was in the middle of the street on her knees crying. "Alice, where is Adam?"

Mrs. Jensen continued sobbing, unresponsive to Aunt Virginia's question. She shook Mrs. Jensen. "Alice, is Adam still inside?"

Alice nodded, "Yes."

Uncle Harold overheard. Without even thinking, he ran past the bucket line through the flaming front door.

Aunt Virginia reacted immediately. "No, Harold, it's too late!"

Mr. Milton held her aunt back from running in after Uncle Harold. Aunt Virginia screamed out pushing against Mr. Milton's arms. "Harold!"

It seemed too long before Mr. Milton was reaching through the door to grab Adam's limp body away from Uncle Harold. Mr. Milton quickly carried Adam into the street away from the building, where Alice snapped into nurse mode to care for his needs. Uncle Harold stumbled into the street where he collapsed. Aunt Virginia took him into her arms, Sarah and her father kneeling next to her. Uncle Harold's face was black from the smoke. He stopped breathing. Aunt Virginia called out, "Alice!"

Mrs. Jensen looked up from her husband who was bent over coughing. She rushed to their assistance, breathing short puffs of breath into his mouth until he coughed and gasped for breath. Sarah breathed in a gulp of air, realizing she had been holding her breath, waiting for her uncle to breathe.

A water brigade still lined the street, pouring water onto the post office, as flames from the boarding house reached higher into the sky. Everyone moved back when glass exploded onto the street below the boarding house. Flames burst through the broken windows, reaching toward the roof. Loud creaking came from inside the building as beams weakened and snapped. Her father and Mr. Milton yelled at everyone to get away because the building was going to collapse.

Sarah ran to the bridge with her father to escape the collapsing building. Two men helped Alice up from the street and hooked their hands under Adam's arms; he was still too overcome to move on his own. Everyone quickly retreated to the bridge. They were all a safe distance away from the boarding house when it collapsed with a great roar, embers and boards flying out over the creek.

As soon as they were able, men gathered in front of the area where the boarding house had stood and began dousing the post office with water in order to save it from the fire. Paint on the side of the building was peeling from the excessive heat; cinders from the collapsed building dusted the roof. Men quickly got up on the roof to sweep it clean of the cinders, pouring more water on the structure.

It was lunchtime when it was declared that the post office was finally safe. It would need new paint and a few roof panels, but it had survived the fire. Everyone was dirty and tired. The Jensens and the few boarders they had been housing were taken to the hotel to rest and recover. The boarding house was a complete loss. The Jensens had lost everything except for the clothes they were wearing.

Uncle Harold had some burns to his face, which Aunt Virginia treated with cool cloths. His hands, which had also sustained burns, were wrapped. Sarah and her father walked home exhausted. Her father walked slower than usual, his previous hunting accident having taken its toll on his body. Sarah worried about him getting sick from too much exertion.

She was still in shock over the extreme actions her uncle had taken to save Mr. Jensen's life. "Father, why would Uncle Harold risk his life to save Mr. Jensen?"

"Sarah, I think Uncle Harold does the right thing regardless of the consequences." Sarah remembered how her uncle had ridden down the mountain after her father's accident, his bare chest exposed to the cold air. He had risked his own health for the life of her father. She was proud of the kind of person her uncle was.

By the time they arrived home, Sarah and her father were too exhausted to celebrate Christmas. They had barely enough energy to tend to the chickens and Duke before going to bed. The Christmas tree in the corner of the living room was the only evidence that Christmas had happened at all.

The next morning Sarah woke up with sore muscles in her arms and neck. She massaged the aching muscles before getting out of bed. Then she remembered the fire and the buckets she had helped pass along.

Her father was already up; a mature blaze roaring in the fireplace. Two tin cups of hot cocoa were on the table, oats boiling on the stove.

Sarah opened her eyes wide when she saw the mugs. "Hot cocoa!" The hot cocoa was a special surprise, something her mother had always served on Christmas morning. She took a big drink of the hot liquid and licked at the foamy mustache on her upper lip.

Her father greeted her with a hug. "Merry Christmas, Sarah."

It didn't matter to Sarah that they were celebrating Christmas a day late. She enjoyed the oatmeal with brown sugar generously sprinkled on top. Her father made her a second tin of hot cocoa to enjoy by the Christmas tree.

He took a package from under the tree and gave it to Sarah. She hadn't even noticed that he had put anything there. She put her tin cup on the floor and took the gift from her father.

It was a large, rectangular package wrapped in brown packing paper. Twine was tied around it twice, finished in a simple bow on top.

"Open it, Sarah!"

She ripped into the paper. Inside was a blue calico dress. She pulled it out and held it against herself. She could see that the sleeves reached her wrists and the bottom of the dress would cover her ankles. She swirled in a circle as she held it against herself. Sarah couldn't wait to wear it.

"I will feel like such a young lady in this! Thank you!" Sarah smiled up at her father. There was something more—underneath the dress was a long grey wool coat for winter. Again the sleeves reached all the way down to her hands. "It's not too short!" This time Sarah hugged her father.

He seemed pleased that she liked her gifts, "I noticed recently you had grown a few inches."

Sarah still had her arms wrapped around her father's neck when he said he had one more gift for her. He disappeared into the bedroom. He returned carrying a brand new pair of lace-up boots in his hands.

She was trying the boots on when someone knocked on the front door. Her father answered it.

"Merry Christmas!" Aunt Virginia greeted her brother with a hug.

Sarah ran to the door. "Merry Christmas, Aunt Virginia!"

Her aunt gave her a basket of muffins.

Sarah took her aunt's hand, "Come in and have hot cocoa with us."

"Thank you Sarah, but I was only stopping by to let you know we are inviting anyone who wants to come to join us at the hotel for stew. After what happened yesterday we could all use a celebration."

Her father spoke immediately. "We'll be there!"

"Come when you're ready, but dinner will be served at noon." Aunt Virginia waved to them as she rushed off.

Her father was already headed out the door to ready the sleigh when she stopped him. "I have a gift for you, too, Father."

He sat down on the stool by the fire. Sarah brought him the gift she had purchased. When he opened it he looked up, surprised. "How did you know I wanted this book?"

She smiled at him.

"Mr. Wagner told me you had been looking at it."

"Sarah, this was very thoughtful of you. Thank you."

After they put away their gifts they readied themselves for dinner with their family at the hotel. Her father hooked Duke up to the sleigh.

Sarah brought extra blankets to the sleigh for the short but cold journey to the hotel.

On the way there, her father looked over at her and smiled. "Sarah, I really enjoyed our Christmas morning together. You are growing up to be such a wonderful young lady." He paused looking at the path ahead of the sleigh.

Sarah didn't know what to say. Her father had never talked to her in this way.

He spoke again. "I'm proud of you Sarah, and I love you very much."

Sarah had a feeling of contentment and love toward her father. Her tears were close to overflowing. She rested her head against her father's warm arm, listening to the sled run smoothly over the snow.

Leia

"*Mother*" by Sarah Richardson

CHAPTER 17

Christmas in Trout Run

Leia stirred in bed, opening her eyes slightly in the darkness before dawn. Light from the fireplace in the front room was flickering in the open space under her bedroom door. She could smell pancakes cooking. It was Christmas morning, the first one without her daughter in fourteen years, and the first without John in seventeen years. She missed them deeply, wondering what their morning was like. She stretched her body out under the covers only to discover how cold it was and she curled up again for warmth. Pulling the thick quilt up to her nose, she sunk deep into her pillow.

A soft knock came to her door. "Leia, may I come in?"

Leia hadn't even answered when the door cracked open. She sat up in bed. "Yes, mother, you may come in."

Her mother came over to her bed holding a hand behind her back. "Leia, I couldn't wait any longer. I knew this would be a difficult morning for you away from your family, so I wanted to help start your day off happy." She pulled her arm out from behind her, "I hope you won't mind this gift."

Caroline placed a wide-eyed black and white kitten in the palm of Leia's hands. It looked like an exact miniature of the pregnant cat Jasmine had been carrying around at the hog butchering. Caroline reached down and hugged her daughter's shoulders to herself. She kissed the top of Leia's head.

"Merry Christmas, Leia. I love you so much."

Leia was completely surprised at the gift. "Thank you, Mother!" She wiped away tears that had quickly come. She laughed. "Goodness, I'm like a child again. I would never have asked for a kitten, but she is perfect!" Leia held the kitten up close to her face, its soft paws pushing against her nose.

Caroline sat at the end of Leia's bed, resting her back against the iron footrest. "Ruby's cat had kittens. Jasmine came over yesterday with this little one, insisting you have her. She named her Nevaeh, which she said is Heaven spelled backwards. She specifically said you could call her Nevi for short. I thought it would be perfect for you."

"Oh Mother, she is perfect! Nevi!"

After breakfast, they spent the day together by the fire with Nevi curled up in a soft blanket near the fireplace.

"Mother, why did you marry father?"

Caroline was quiet for a while before she answered. "I was seventeen when, one afternoon, I was walking home from church and saw a young man taming a wild mustang, riding him for a few seconds before being bucked off into the dirt. When he stood up, he brushed off his hat against his buckskin chaps. Just before placing his hat back on his head, he looked up, his eyes meeting mine. I recognized him. He had been thrown out of school the year before for being too rowdy. I had never noticed him before, but now, in that corral, he looked like a man with a wild spirit, a man destined for adventure." Caroline rocked in her chair. "I was young. I didn't see him for what he really was under that tough exterior."

"When did you discover his temper?"

"We courted for a year. My father vocalized his disapproval of the match but gave permission against his better judgment. Your father and I went away for three days to some local springs to marry and honeymoon. We moved into a house the railroad provided for us with his job. He often came home late, drunk. One day I left to help a neighbor out with her sick children. When he came home to an empty house, no dinner on the table, and floors in need of mopping, he came looking for me. I had left a note on the table as to where I was. When he arrived at the neighbor's house, he insisted I was needed at home. As soon as we arrived home, he threw me inside. My body slammed into the dinner table. When I cried out, reaching toward my bruised side, he hit me across the face.

He yelled at me. 'Mrs. Smith can take care of her own sick children! I expect dinner on the table when I come home.'"

Caroline paused for a moment. "I'm surprised at the emotion I feel, even now, telling you this."

Leia was teary-eyed. She tried to imagine the fear her mother experienced as a young bride. "What did you do, Mother?"

"I didn't do anything, Leia. I was terrified. Pride kept me from running home to my parents. Within months I was pregnant with you. I did everything I could to stay out of his way. I feared for our future but hoped having a child would tame him. It did not."

Leia walked to her mother's rocker and knelt down beside it to look up at her. "I'm sorry, Mother."

Caroline reached a hand toward Leia, taking her hands between her own. "Leia, God has given us each other again. I'm sorry for you, for what your father did to you, for what he did to me. I love you Leia, more than I have ever loved anyone in my life. Having you here is an answer to years of prayer."

Nevi continued her winter nap by the fire while Caroline and Leia talked into the evening.

CHAPTER 18

Spring

In the days following the fire it was determined that an overturned oil lamp on the first floor of the boarding house had lit a curtain on fire. The Jensens, along with the displaced boarders, stayed at the hotel. Alice worked in the kitchen in return for room and board. Once Adam recovered from his burns he helped Harold in the barn and with repairs around the property. Alice had visible bruises on her arms and chin. Adam was quiet for a week after the accident. Then one day while he was in the barn with Harold, Adam finally asked,

"Why did you go into that burning building for me, Harold? You have a family to think about."

"I couldn't stand by and let you die, Adam."

Adam's face revealed the torment he was feeling about the fire. "How would you feel, Harold, if you had known when you rescued me that I was passed out from drinking? I fought with Alice the night before, and although I can't remember much, I'm sure I hit her—a few times—and more than likely knocked that oil lamp over when I passed out. If you had known what kind of lowlife I really am, would you still have gone in after me, Harold?"

Harold didn't even hesitate. "Yes, Adam."

Adam didn't say anything more. Over time, Alice and Adam told Virginia and Harold about their struggles with Adam's drinking and abuse. He had begun drinking in the early years of their marriage when they lost their only child to influenza. The fire disturbed Adam. He wanted to change his ways. Virginia asked them if they had any relatives who would help them. Alice decided to write her sister in Wellsboro.

After letters were exchanged, the Jensens decided that in the spring, after Virginia's baby was born, they would move to Wellsboro to live with Alice's sister. Her brother-in-law was a director at the Wellsboro hospital where she would be able to work as a nurse. They could start over while having family close by to help them.

Alice worked tirelessly alongside Sarah and Virginia until the baby came on February 6, a cold, snowy Monday morning. The labor lasted throughout the day when finally at 10 o'clock that night she delivered a tiny baby boy whom she and Harold named Joseph.

Alice made sure Virginia rested the following week. Sarah took turns helping with baby Joseph. Mason and Janine were fascinated with the new little one. Janine liked to smell his head and touch his soft baby face. Sarah quietly told her all about his little toes and fingers as Janine touched each one.

With Sarah staying all day at the restaurant and her father working, time passed without them realizing they weren't talking as often as they had been. They were too exhausted from their work.

One evening, in the barn, John noticed three little chicks had hatched and another was pecking out of its shell. He rushed inside to let Sarah know. They watched the little one work its way through the shell. Its wet feathers clung to its skinny little body. John brought all of them inside with the mother hen to rest in the warmth of the fire. By morning the wet feathers were clean and fuzzy. Spring was on its way.

Sarah was relieved when March ended with warm breezes and gentle rain that thawed the ice and snow. She was ready for the snow on the mountains to melt. After two days of rain, the weight of the water sitting on the ice in Pine Creek, along with the pressure of the moving water underneath, finally started to crack the ice. Sarah was in the kitchen with Mrs. Jensen when they both heard loud popping and cracking echo off the hillside. Aunt Virginia came down the stairs with baby Joseph wrapped tightly in blankets. She looked happy to be walking around with him in her arms.

Uncle Harold came to the kitchen to alert them of the impending ice flow. "The ice is ready to break up. I'll get Mason and Janine. We can watch the ice from above the splash dam."

Sarah gladly hung her apron on a hook by the door before putting on her scarf, hat, coat, and boots. Uncle Harold carried Janine. She wrapped her arms wrapped tightly around his neck.

Sarah held Mason's hand as they hurried along the path through the yard over the footbridge that crossed an icy spring, to an area above the splash dam.

Another loud boom echoed off the mountains. Janine clung more tightly to her father. He whispered in her ear, "It's the ice breaking on the creek, Janine, so spring can come to make the flowers bloom."

Sarah hurried to the edge of the riverbank; Mason matched her stride the whole time. Cracks were branching across the ice when suddenly the ice exploded, violently rising up and pushing forward. Huge slabs of ice came from upstream wedging under unbroken ice, driving large slabs straight up into the air. One jagged square of ice as tall as a house was forced upright then slammed against the splash dam. The icy water pushed against the slab, splashing around it to find a way over the edge of the dam.

Uncle Harold stepped back taking Aunt Virginia's arm. "Time to back up. The water level is rising."

They rushed up the hill high enough to escape the rising water and ice.

Mason was jumping up and down and pointing at the hotel yard. "Look!"

Ice was flowing into the yard of the hotel, surrounding the tree trunks at the water's edge, and pushing ice as far as the porch railing on the restaurant.

"We will have to take a higher trail home," Uncle Harold said, but didn't sound worried.

The creek became temporarily jammed with broken ice. The flow of water halted. It was eerily silent until water from upstream suddenly and forcefully pushed the ice downstream. The ice was replaced with swift brown water. The water level quickly dropped leaving behind ice haphazardly suspended on river shrubs and low hanging branches. Some of the large ice slabs lodged in the muddy creek banks, standing taller than the homes in whose yards they rested. The restaurant yard was impassible, stacked high with layers of stranded ice.

As Sarah walked back to the hotel, she looked up at the mountaintop. A trail of smoke was rising from a chimney on the Stephens' ranch where Matthew lived. The breaking of the ice meant the mountain paths would soon be clear. It wouldn't be long before she saw Matthew again.

The day after the ice flow was the day Mr. and Mrs. Jensen left for Wellsboro. A number of townspeople, dressed in Sunday best, came to the train station to see them off. Sarah wore the long blue dress her father had given her for Christmas.

Virginia packed sandwiches for the Jensens to take on their trip, wrapping them in a basket with venison jerky. Sarah added a little bag of marigold seeds to the basket, saved from her mother's garden in Williamsport. The train came north from Jersey Shore and stopped in front of the station. The Jensens waited to board until the supplies were unloaded from the cargo cars, and then they stepped onboard, waving goodbye to everyone.

Sarah and her father watched the train until the smoke disappeared around the bend of the mountain.

"Time to go, Sarah. I have some supplies to pick up at the general store before heading home."

A tall man in a dark grey suit was standing next to supply crates on the loading platform. The rim of his hat was hiding his eyes. When Sarah and her father walked by, the gentleman lifted his gaze, his eyes meeting Sarah's.

Sarah stopped. She was looking into eyes she would never forget: the eyes of Reverend Claythorn!

CHAPTER 19

A New Reverend

Sarah could see the shock in Reverend Claythorn's face when he recognized them. When she saw her father notice him, she thought they might say something to each other but instead her father turned and continued on his way to the general store.

Once inside the general store, Sarah realized her hands were clenched into fists. She wondered why Reverend Claythorn was in Slate Run.

In the store Sarah tried to focus on what she needed for home. She couldn't remember if they were out of sugar or flour. Sarah wished she had made a list. Her father waited at the counter for Mr. Wagner to finish an order for Oscar Milton.

"John, I'll be with you as soon as I finish with Oscar's order."

Sarah could overhear Mr. Wagner talking with Oscar. "I'm pretty anxious to meet him. The headquarters gave him high recommendations. He did some missionary work with the Indians out west for a while. His most recent work was starting a church in Williamsport."

Oscar agreed with Mr. Wagner. "It has been too long since we have had a regular preacher at the church. I was told he is a passionate speaker."

When Mr. Wagner helped her father with his order he asked him about the reverend. "John, did you know Reverend Claythorn in Williamsport?"

Sarah was looking at a basket of yarn when she overheard the question. Her shoulder muscles tensed.

"Yes, I attended the church he started in Williamsport."

Mr. Wagner was enthusiastic at this information. "What can you tell us about him?"

Mr. Wagner and Oscar gave her father their full attention.

"He was a passionate speaker, but I didn't know him that well." Sarah could tell that her father's answer disappointed them.

As soon as her father's order was finished, he made a motion to leave. "Good day, gentlemen."

Sarah was glad they were leaving. A fine rain filled the air, making the road muddy and rutted. Sarah's thoughts were anxious. She and her father could not escape what had happened in Williamsport; it had followed them here.

Sarah went to the barn to feed the chicks. She scattered food for the hen and rooster. The little chicks followed her around, pecking at the grain on the barn floor. When she finished raking the hay on the floor and filling Duke's feed basket, she picked up his brush. With long firm strokes she pushed the dirt and rain from his coat.

Her father was behind the house splitting wood. The pile of wood against the house would last until early summer. She knew he was chopping more than wood. He was angry. She started brushing out Duke's blond tail. "No good will come of this."

Reverend Claythorn was the most frequent subject of discussion among the customers at the restaurant.

Aunt Virginia talked about Reverend Claythorn while they were cooking. Sarah wondered if they should have told her aunt and uncle why her mother ran away.

"Sarah, things are much better with Reverend Claythorn here. Last week he gave the most passionate sermon on the lost sheep."

Sarah nodded her head at the appropriate times but didn't hear most of what her aunt said. Her aunt continued on. "I can't believe that he isn't married. He's a good-looking man. It's unfortunate for him he moved to a town of all men."

Sarah's head was pounding by the time she left the restaurant. Evenings at home weren't the same anymore either. Sarah and her father spent their evenings in silence. He never took out the harmonica anymore. The house was quiet.

As temperatures warmed Sarah began hiking on the mountain again. Often, with a drawing tablet in hand, she would find her favorite rock or meadow in which to quietly draw or listen to the wind in the trees. Sarah had a feeling of weariness in her soul. She thought about her aunt's talk about seeing joy in the common hours, but all Sarah could feel right now was that there was no good left in her life. She drew a picture of the white church by the Susquehanna River: a gleaming white building bordered by raging waters.

CHAPTER 20

What Went Wrong?

When John split all the available wood, he started making repairs on the fence around the corral. He could hear Sarah at night crying out from her dreams. In the evenings he kept his hands busy whittling wood by the fireplace while Sarah drew or studied from her schoolbooks. She reminded him of Mary, in her expressions and movements. He was full of regret at what had happened to their family.

At first it had been easy to blame everything on Mary, but he knew he had his own part in letting their marriage fall apart. Now that Reverend Claythorn walked the streets of Slate Run, John was confronted everyday with what had happened. While he whittled in the evenings he thought about the early days of their marriage, of Sarah being born, building their home, helping at the church, and how Reverend Claythorn entered their lives.

Two summers ago Reverend Claythorn had arrived in Williamsport, having just returned from his missionary work in Kansas with the Indians. Shortly after his arrival in Williamsport, Reverend Claythorn came to John and Jacob's Lumber Mill to find some men who were willing to help raise a big tent for revival meetings. John had seen many preachers come into town for "revival meetings." He had watched people make commitments to change their lives only to return to their old ways once the meetings were over. He had never gotten involved with revival meetings until Reverend Claythorn came into the mill that day. The reverend walked up to John, looked him right in the eyes. "John Richardson, I need a man like you around. I have heard good things about the kind of person you are."

John was proud of his reputation in town; he wondered if Reverend Claythorn would care that he wasn't a religious man.

Reverend Claythorn continued, "Can I count on you to help with the tent-raising, to encourage people to be at the meetings? People respect you—they will follow you."

John started to explain that he didn't go to revival meetings, "Reverend Claythorn—"

Reverend Claythorn released his hand, smiling. "See you down at the river on Saturday for the tent-raising. Services begin Sunday night. This town could use some religion."

John wasn't sure how it had happened, but he was at the tent-raising at dawn Saturday morning. When Reverend Claythorn said something, people followed. His sermons were loud, fiery expositions. People came forward by the dozens every service to be saved. Money filled the offering plates. Everyone was talking about the new reverend.

When the cold temperatures of fall began to creep in, Reverend Claythorn told his congregation God had revealed to him a church would be built right here on the banks of the Susquehanna River.

Building began that week with John in charge. John spent his hours away from the mill at the building project, sometimes early before work, sometimes into the dark of night by the light of lanterns. Mary and Sarah began eating dinner without him. Weeks went by when he only came home to sleep. He realized now he had abandoned his family because he felt important working at the church. It had cost him what he valued most.

CHAPTER 21

The Panther

The evenings of early spring were damp and dark. Rain often came down in fine soaking sheets. One evening, just after Sarah had placed steaming bowls of stew on the table, her father came home from the office looking alarmed.

"Sarah, I will take care of Duke and the chickens tonight. I want you to stay inside."

She was frightened by the tone of his voice. "What's wrong, Father?"

"On the way home from the office, I decided to cross the creek instead of taking the bridge. Duke was acting unusual. When we neared the creek bank, he stomped the ground as if he didn't want to cross the stream. I wasn't sure if his leg was bothering him or if he smelled something, so I scanned the creek banks carefully. Although it was dusk, I could see a large dog wading midstream down from where we were. As the dog looked up, I realized I was looking at a panther."

Sarah's eyes widened. "What did you do?"

"I stood quietly on the bank for a few minutes not moving a single muscle as I watched him. Although he looked right at me, he seemed distracted, his eyes darting quickly away toward the meadow on the other side of the creek. A dozen deer stood in the tall grass of the meadow eating, and taking turns watching for predators. When the panther began crossing the creek in a crouched position, I knew he wasn't interested in Duke or me. My new concern was the fact that the field where the deer were grazing edges our property. The panther is hunting too close for me to feel safe letting you go to the barn at night anymore."

Before sitting at the table her father hung his gun above the coat hooks next to the door. Sarah put two tins of milk by each bowl of stew.

He tried to comfort her. "Duke and the chickens will be fine in the barn. I secured the latch on the barn door. After dinner I will take care of feeding them."

That night while sitting by the fire her father reminded her to be careful when she was in the woods. "And it's never a good idea to be in the woods at dusk when panthers are most likely to be hunting."

She had never worried about being attacked by a panther in Williamsport. Sarah didn't like the panther being so close.

Sarah worked long days at the hotel with her aunt. Aunt Virginia often looked exhausted from caring for baby Joseph. He cried a lot. Sarah could see the worry in her aunt's eyes when she was with Joseph. Whenever her aunt needed rest, she took Joseph in her arms. He felt fragile.

Yellow daffodils were blooming along the back patio of the hotel. On nice days the doors to the back patio were opened to allow fresh air in. The long patio was lined with slanted seating chairs her uncle had built. The chairs were filled with woodhicks enjoying a pipe or telling stories. The green lawn sloped down to the creek, and small remnants of the ice flow were still sheltered in shadows against tree trunks. Often in the early morning, just after she would arrive, Sarah would see deer grazing on the grass. It was not unusual to see a bear or bobcat drinking from the creek at dusk.

One afternoon a little hummingbird mistakenly flew into the restaurant. It exhausted itself trying to find its way out. When it rested on a windowsill near the kitchen Sarah quickly scooped it up in her hand. She kept her hands cupped over the tiny bird until she stepped outside. When she opened her hands, the confused hummingbird sat for a moment raising its little eyes up at her. Then it was gone.

On the same day that she had released the hummingbird, Reverend Claythorn came into the restaurant for lunch. Her aunt seemed to have things under control in the kitchen, so she asked if she could leave early to hike in the woods. That was partly true. She did want to hike, but most of all she didn't want to be around when Reverend Claythorn was there.

"Yes, of course Sarah. You have been working tirelessly helping me out since Joseph was born."

Sarah assured her aunt she would be back to help with breakfast in the morning.

Her aunt hugged her goodbye. "See you tomorrow."

Sarah ran home to grab her satchel of drawing pencils and paper. The sun had reached its highest point in the sky. The water level in the creek was low so Sarah crossed the water through the rapids. She had learned to master walking through the rapids. She knew if she looked down too much while crossing the creek the movement of the water would make her dizzy. She had to watch her step because the rocks were so uneven, but Sarah made sure to glance up at the hill occasionally to gather her bearings. She held her dress up to her knees so it wouldn't get too wet. On the far shore, Sarah sat on a boulder to put her shoes back on before hiking.

Sarah found her favorite meadow on the mountain filled with clover and yellow flowers. She took her blanket from her satchel and spread it out over a clover patch. She put her pencils and tablet in the center of the blanket where she laid belly down to draw a picture of her mother. The birds were singing in great number and the warmth of the sun on her back eventually lulled her into resting on her back and gazing at the blue sky. She breathed deeply. It was so peaceful here Sarah felt like she could forget about her problems.

She didn't realize she had fallen asleep until she was awakened by the snap of a twig nearby. She sat up, the bell around her necklace jingling with the movement. She was disoriented, not sure what had woken her up. Sarah surveyed the woods around her. It was unusually quiet, not even the birds were singing. She hurriedly put her shoes on, but didn't lace them up. Standing up slowly she looked around her more closely. A movement from the side caught her eyes. In a patch of ferns a few yards away, she could see the coat of a light brown panther crouching, his tail twitching back and forth. As soon as she saw him she started to run, ignoring every warning she had ever heard about running. The panther sprang forward, landing on the edge of her blanket. It sniffed briefly at the sandwich Sarah had left behind before gulping it down. She continued running, her heart beating fast. The panther resumed racing toward Sarah. A small rock caught her foot and she fell forward, her hands hitting the ground hard as she tried to break her fall. The panther screamed behind her as he pounced on Sarah pushing her over as she tried to stand up. The panther was over her, his hot breath in her face. Futilely she punched the panther's snout. It sunk its teeth into her arm. Then suddenly something hit the panther, driving it away from her. She scrambled to her feet to run. Before she had gotten very far the panther screamed again. A shot rang out.

She stopped to see what had happened, her lungs gasping for breath. A man was dismounting from his horse. He turned toward her to see if she was all right. When Sarah saw that her rescuer was Reverend Claythorn, she ran down the mountain as if the panther was still pursuing her.

By the time Sarah reached the restaurant, she was faint from the loss of blood. Her aunt cleaned the wounds on her arm and stitched the bite marks.

Her father ran into the kitchen while Aunt Virginia was working on Sarah's arm. Mason had run to the lumber company to tell her father what had happened. She heard later that when Mason out of breath, had relayed the incident, her father immediately left for the hotel, not mindful if Mason was keeping up with him.

Aunt Virginia had to work hard to persuade her brother that Sarah was fine and that angels must have been watching over his daughter who somehow survived a panther attack. Before Sarah could explain how she was able to get away from the panther, a commotion outside caught their attention. From the kitchen window they could see a group of men headed toward the parsonage.

Her father stood near the window, curious. "What could that be about?"

Sarah knew he would soon find out what had happened on the mountain. "Reverend Claythorn killed the panther. They are probably all gawking at the body of the panther."

She saw her father tense up.

Her aunt was surprised at the news. "Reverend Claythorn saved you from the panther?"

The question was asked, but Sarah could not bring herself to say that Reverend Claythorn had been her rescuer.

Sarah was living in a nightmare. On her way to the hotel the next morning, she passed the parsonage. A number of men were helping Reverend Claythorn cure the panther skin with salts before putting it on a stretcher for drying. All that week she walked by the skin setting in front of the parsonage. Just when people had settled down about Reverend Claythorn, they were all anxious to hear the story about the panther. Everyone was talking about what had happened on the mountain except Sarah and her father. In the post office, she overheard Reverend Claythorn talking to a group of people gathered in front of the building.

"I woke up that morning with a strong feeling God was telling me to visit the Stephens' ranch on the mountain. If I had ignored the calling of God, that young girl would not be with us today."

He entertained people with the account of how he had hit the panther with a stick just after it had pounced on the girl. When it ran after her again, he shot it. People were enthralled with the tale and in awe of its teller. Sarah was angry that Reverend Claythorn had been her rescuer.

One day, in the general store, Mr. Wagner asked her about what happened. "What did you think when you saw the panther coming after you?"

It became quiet in the store as a group of woodhicks paused to hear her answer. Her face reddened. Not knowing what else to do, she ran out of the store.

Mr. Wagner watched her as she ran out. "Poor thing, she must be in shock over such an ordeal."

She heard the comment before she made it out the door. Sarah thought it was just as well if everyone believed she was in shock. Avoiding the hotel for too much longer wasn't realistic, so she regretfully came in after three days of being away. She knew her aunt needed her help, especially with Joseph not doing so well. She decided the best thing to do was to bring up the subject herself.

Sarah was tying on her apron by the stove. "Aunt Virginia, I know you have heard the story of the panther—"

Her aunt nodded her head. "Yes, and I have been concerned about you, especially when you didn't make it in the last few days. Are you doing okay? Is your arm healing up without infection?"

Sarah looked right at her aunt. "The whole incident with the panther has given me nightmares. I'm not comfortable talking about what happened yet."

Aunt Virginia understood. "I'm just glad to have you back. You're like a daughter to me. There will be no talk of panthers in this kitchen."

Sarah was relieved but not surprised her aunt would understand. She guessed her aunt must have also talked to Mason and Janine because they never asked her again about the panther.

Weeks passed and the panther skin still hung on the stretcher in front of the parsonage. One day she scooped up a clod of fresh mud from the road and slung it at the skin. "Stupid panther!" Reverend Claythorn opened his front door just in time to see her running toward home. She would have been surprised at the expression on his face. It wasn't anger. It was sadness, like that of a man who was carrying a heavy burden.

Leia

"*Mother*" by *Sarah Richardson*

CHAPTER 22

Soul Spring

In early April Leia saw a purple crocus breaking through the surface of the snow near her mother's front door. Within the week a single flower had grown to an expanding clump. Snowy pathways were melting into soggy mud. By the time Easter came, yellow daffodils were in abundance. Most days were still dark with drizzling rain, but the temperatures were slowly rising.

On Easter Sunday Leia found herself walking through the doors of the church for the first time since leaving Revival Bible Church in Williamsport. Her mother had invited her to come to Easter service. It was a rare sunny day and people, dressed in their best spring clothes, were gathered in groups in front of the church. Her mother introduced her to some of the ladies, most of whom she had met at the hog butchering.

One elderly lady remembered her, "Leia! It is so good to see you here."

The ladies were kind, making small talk with her, but Leia could scarcely concentrate. She headed through the double white doors with her mother. Once her eyes adjusted to the inside, she was surprised how much it resembled the church in Williamsport. When the congregation started singing she closed her eyes, barely composed.

Shall we gather at the river—

The congregation was singing the song that had been sung the morning she left Williamsport. The totality of her loss filled her soul. John's face came to her mind: the face of the man she deeply loved and had completely deceived. She wished to be held once again by her husband. She missed her daughter. It was all gone. Tears began to slide down her face. When her mother reached over to hold her hand, she cried more.

The reverend stood up behind the little wooden pulpit, placing his Bible on it. Leia forced her eyes open. The minister was an elderly man who, she had heard, spent his younger years preaching in New York City before returning to preach in the mountains he loved. Today he read from the book of John about Jesus being killed on the cross. He explained how all have sinned therefore removing the ability to have friendship with God. His message was confirming to her the idea that God was not interested in her anymore because of her sin. The reverend continued. He explained how Jesus took the burden of sin upon himself. He sacrificed his only son Jesus to pay the price of the sin committed.

Then he read about Mary coming to Jesus' tomb, three days after Jesus' death, in the early morning hours. Leia paid close attention when he mentioned Mary Magdalene. Leia felt she could identify with her, a woman known at one time for her sin. When the story continued the Reverend spoke of how Mary Magdalene was distraught to find Jesus gone from the tomb. Jesus came to her to speak her name, "Mary". Mary knew immediately it was Jesus. Jesus was no longer dead; he had risen from the grave. The reverend explained that Jesus conquered death so we could be free from the burdens we were carrying.

Leia knew she couldn't carry the burden of her hate for her father or the shame of her marriage any longer. When her breathing became difficult, she knew she needed to get outside. Leia loosened the grasp on her mother's hand and stood up. There were five people between her and the aisle, a detail she hadn't noticed until she was standing up in the middle of a silent church service.

She was close to completely losing control of her emotions. Leia moved quickly past long cotton dresses and shoes that blocked her way. People pulled their feet back as she exited, but Leia took one women by surprise. As she stumbled on the woman's pointy lace-up boot, the woman gasped in shock. When Leia stumbled she fell toward Ruby, hitting her on the shoulder. Leia's hat fell off onto the floor. As she kept herself from falling completely onto Ruby by extending a hand to the back of the pew behind Ruby, Ruby looked up at Leia's eyes. Leia was gasping back her cries. She reached the end of the pew and raced toward the double doors at the back of the church.

Once she reached the bottom of the stairs outside, she picked up her skirt and ran toward the trees at the edge of a large field. She heard the voice of her father in her mind: *You are worthless, Leia. You can't do anything right.* Then her own thoughts condemned her—she believed she was worthless. But the reverend had said that God loved her, that she was already forgiven. Her legs were sore from the run and her lungs spent of air. She fell into the tall grass at the edge of the woods. Lying on the ground, she wept out loud.

Ruby and Caroline followed Leia outside shortly after her flight from the church. They watched Leia run until she dropped down into the tall grass. Caroline started down the steps to go after her but Ruby reached for her arm, "Caroline, can I go ahead of you?"

Caroline looked at Ruby confused. She wondered: shouldn't she herself be the one to go after her daughter?

Ruby spoke again, "She's your daughter, Caroline, but you know you can trust me." Caroline remembered back to the day when she had given her own burdens to God. Ruby was the one sitting with her at the kitchen table praying with her. Caroline longed to comfort her grieving daughter, but she wondered if maybe a mother's comfort isn't what she needed at the moment. She looked at Ruby, "Go to her." Ruby hastened down the stairs toward the field. Caroline watched, holding the stair railing tightly as if to keep herself from going too.

Leia couldn't stop herself from crying or her body from shaking. She was nauseous from the emotions that were overwhelming her. When she heard the rustling of grass behind her, she paused and sniffled back her tears for a moment. She looked up as Ruby approached her. When Ruby sat next to her and took Leia into her arms, Leia started crying again. Ruby rocked her back and forth like she would her little Jasmine, brushing the hair away from Leia's wet cheeks.

Ruby's words came softly and without condemnation, "God has already offered to take your burden Leia. Just give it to Him."

Leia looked at her friend, "How?"

Ruby held Leia's head against her shoulder, "He already knows what's in your heart, just talk to him. Ask God to forgive you for what you have done. Ask Him to take your burdens."

Leia was beginning to calm down but still felt conflicted inside. She sat up. "Ruby, I have nothing to offer God. I've never done anything right in my life. All I could think about in church was how I turned my back on my husband and my daughter. I don't deserve what God is offering."

Ruby smiled at her, "God's offer only requires that you take it. Leia, God made you and everything he makes is worth more than gold. You need to see yourself through His eyes, not the eyes of your father or through the wrong you have done. God loves you."

Leia was emptied of anything she could do to relieve the heaviness she felt, except to let God take it. She fell face-down on the ground again. Her lips moved soundlessly as she said her first prayer to God. All the years of hate and sorrow were going away. Leia felt like she could breathe, and for the first time in her life she felt a sense of hope. When she sat up again she saw her mother approaching. Leia stood up to reach for her, "Mother! I'm forgiven!"

Now Caroline wept. "My Leia. My daughter."

Ruby stepped back as the two embraced. Caroline looked over her daughter's shoulders to Ruby and motioned for her to join them. The three women, standing in the tall grass under the light of the warm spring sun, hugged and cried tears of joy in a tight circle of arms.

Over the next few weeks, Leia and her mother talked constantly. Caroline told Leia about life with Ben and how life was since his death. Leia told her about her own family. "Mother, I miss Sarah and John. But I don't see how things can be made right again."

Caroline was encouraging. "God is in the business of making things right again; talk to Him about it."

One afternoon while they were gathering flowers from the garden, Leia spoke out loud the idea she had been pondering, "Mother, would you consider leaving Trout Run to live with me—with my family? I might be asking a lot of my family to not only take me back, but to also bring in someone they don't know—but we have lost too many years already, Mother."

"Leia, I don't want to lose you again either."

Leia put a small purple flower in her mother's hair, just behind her left ear.

"I don't know how things will go in Williamsport," Leia said, "but it's time for me to return home. I want to tell John and Sarah how much I love them."

They would spend the next two months closing up the house in Slate Run. Leia purchased tickets for the stagecoach ride to Williamsport for June 1. She was nervous about returning home to Williamsport. There were many times when she changed her mind, determined it was a bad idea. She wasn't sure John could forgive her. At times she would feel panic coming over her when she thought of the mess she had left behind. She prayed constantly that somehow she would be able to return home. She longed to be with her family again. But there was something else left undone. She had to tell her mother about her name.

CHAPTER 23

Baby Joseph

April blended into May under dark clouds. Sarah couldn't remember the last time she had seen the sunlight. The streets in town were rutted with mud. On her way to the hotel she passed a wagon whose wheel had been sucked into a deep puddle. A group of men were trying to push the wagon up out of the mud. She did her best to hold her skirts high enough to avoid getting too dirty as she walked the dirt road. It seemed like she was washing clothes all the time because of the weather.

By the time she reached the hotel her boots were shin-deep in mud. She carefully stepped inside the kitchen onto the mat her aunt had put down to protect the floorboards. A wide tin bucket sat next to the mat for wet shoes. She slipped off her boots and placed them in the tin. When she reached for an apron near the stove she realized the kitchen was dark. The stove was cold to her touch. All the cooking pots were still hanging from their hooks above the sink where Sarah had hung them the night before.

The floor felt cold through her stockings as she entered the restaurant area. It was dark and quiet. She proceeded into the parlor. It was also dark so she continued through the dining area toward the staircase to the family quarters. She rounded the corner of the balustrade where she found her niece and nephew sitting quietly. They were huddled together, still in their nightclothes. Sarah was alarmed. She reached toward them calmly whispering to Mason, "Where's your mother and father?"

Mason looked up the stairs where a sound of soft crying could be heard. She ran up the stairs and down the hallway to an open doorway. Her aunt was sitting in the rocking chair next to baby Joseph's crib. Uncle Harold was standing beside the crib looking down at the dead body of his son.

A small pine box was carried between two men from the little church to the hill behind the hotel where the cemetery lay. The sun was making a rare appearance between puffy white clouds. The sawmill shut down for the funeral. Everyone was attending the service for little Joseph. Reverend Claythorn walked in front of the casket, leading the way to the small cemetery that rested in the shade of tall pines against the base of the mountain behind the hotel. A stone sat above a freshly dug hole.

Joseph Plumb
February 6, 1889 – May 10, 1889

When the procession of people walking to the cemetery stopped, Sarah looked down at her new lace-up boots. Reverend Claythorn was talking. Aunt Virginia was leaning against Uncle Harold. Sarah never looked up from her boots during the ceremony. A light breeze blew through the Boston ferns growing in the shade of the pines, and a daddy long-legs spider was crawling around at the base of the gravestone.

Reverend Claythorn stopped speaking. The small box was lowered into the hole. First Uncle Harold, then Aunt Virginia, tossed handfuls of dirt on the casket. The soft soil made an odd sound as it hit the wood.

Sarah held the tears back, her throat aching with the effort. After the service she lingered while her father helped some men fill in the hole. Her aunt and uncle headed back to the hotel with Mason and Janine.

The week following the funeral was again rainy. Aunt Virginia was quiet as they worked in the kitchen. Sarah didn't know what to say, but knew she could at least help with the work. One morning after breakfast had been cleaned up, her aunt went upstairs for a little rest. Mason was on the porch building a cabin with some miniature logs her uncle made.

She looked for Janine whom she found sitting at the piano in the dining room. Janine was brushing her fingers over the tops of the smooth, ivory keys. Sarah's mother had taught her to play piano a few years ago. She hadn't kept up the lessons, but she still found enjoyment playing tunes occasionally. When Sarah sat down on the bench Janine recognized her breathing. She smiled in Sarah's direction.

"Sawah?"

Brushing her hands over the keys, Sarah thought about her mother. She placed Janine's hands over her own as she played a few notes. Sarah looked down at Janine's tiny fingers trying to imagine what it must feel like to touch the smooth texture of ivory without the aid of vision.

Sarah picked up the pace, playing a crazy, lilting tune. When she finished it, she told her niece, "That was *Polly Wolly Doodle.*"

Janine could barely understand the title. "Polly who?"

"*Polly Wolly Doodle.*"

Janine giggled trying to say it herself, "Polly Wolly oodle!"

Sarah played it again, this time singing the words with the tune:

"Oh, I went down South
For to see my Sal
Sing Polly wolly doodle all the day
My Sal, she is

A spunky gal
Sing Polly wolly doodle all the day
Fare thee well,
Fare thee well,
Fare thee well my fairy fay,
For I'm going to Louisiana,
For to see my Susy-anna
Singing Polly wolly doodle all the day."

They both laughed together. Sarah slowed her playing down again, placing Janine's hand back on her own. Gently Sarah played the notes to "Mary Had a Little Lamb". She played it several times before placing one of Janine's hands directly on the keys. Sarah pushed Janine's fingers down on the correct notes. Janine concentrated on every movement and was able to repeat most of the song on her own.

Virginia had been listening from the kitchen and later told her niece, "Thank you, for giving Janine extra attention today; you are a gift to all of us."

When she returned home that night, Sarah's head was full of the kind words her aunt had said. Those were the kind of words she missed hearing from her mother. She was missing her so much. The only tangible piece of her Sarah had was her mother's Bible that rested under her drawing pad on the nightstand. She hadn't opened the Bible at all but had kept it next to her for comfort. Tonight she sat down on her bed, thumbing through the thin pages. The Bible fell open to a page with a dried rose pressed in the middle, presumably one her father had given her mother at some time. She carefully picked up the rose to read the words on the page beneath it,

Charity suffereth long, and is kind; charity envieth not; charity vaunteth not itself, is not puffed up, ⁵ Doth not behave itself unseemly, seeketh not her own, is not easily provoked, thinketh no evil; ⁶ Rejoiceth not in iniquity, but rejoiceth in the truth; ⁷ Beareth all things, believeth all things, hopeth all things, endureth all things. ⁸ Charity never faileth.

She put the rose back in the Bible and fell asleep thinking about the mysterious words, "Charity never faileth."

In the weeks that followed, Virginia remained quieter than usual. Sarah knew she was still grieving over baby Joseph. She kept busy helping her aunt at the hotel and continued teaching Janine "Mary Had a Little Lamb" on the piano.

One evening her father talked to her as they sat by the fireplace. "Sarah, you're doing the right thing helping Aunt Virginia in the kitchen and spending time with Janine. You're showing them love is the best thing for their healing hearts."

"I didn't think I was being that helpful. I don't know what to say to comfort Aunt Virginia."

John looked at his daughter. "Love is stronger than words, Sarah." She remembered again the words she had read earlier in her mother's Bible: *Charity never faileth.*

That night she dreamed of her mother. When she awoke with a start she said her first prayer. It was for her mother and for her family. Somehow, in all this pain, she hoped God was listening.

Two days later things seemed to get worse. She had taken a break after serving lunch at the hotel, to check for mail at the post office. On her way back she was looking across the street toward the hotel, when something made her stop to take a closer look. Aunt Virginia was outside the kitchen door in her apron, greeting Reverend Claythorn. As he was talking to her he reached forward, taking her hands in his. It appeared that he was consoling her. Sarah felt herself burn inside, watching Reverend Claythorn hold Aunt Virginia's hands.

Later that day as she cooked in the kitchen with her aunt, she was quiet about what she had seen. As each hour in the kitchen went by, her anger toward Reverend Claythorn grew. With each potato she skinned, she gained the determination to finally confront Reverend Claythorn.

Sarah was so determined to face him she forgot to say goodbye to her aunt when she left the hotel. Reverend Claythorn's parsonage was behind the church on the way home. Once there, she stood on the porch of the parsonage wondering if she should confront him. She cleared her throat with renewed determination. She knocked. The door opened and there stood Reverend Claythorn, a shocked expression on his face.

She didn't let herself pause as she loudly addressed him. "Stay away from my aunt, Reverend Claythorn! You have done enough damage—to my family—already!" She stood in the doorway, having more to say, but not able to speak above the emotions that were making her heart pound. When tears started to come, she ran from the porch ashamed she had lost her courage.

CHAPTER 24

Spring Drive

Rain and melting snow were increasing the water levels in Pine Creek. It was time to push lumber south to the boom in Williamsport. Hundreds of woodhicks came into town to ready for the spring drive. Four large rectangular boxes built on top of rafts, called arks, were quickly assembled. One ark would house the woodhicks; another would act as a kitchen-dining area; a third would board the horses for the journey. Sarah's father had an extra ark built to house Sarah and him. Sarah was surprised and excited she was allowed to go on the drive. They planned on returning to Slate Run on the train.

The morning of the drive, Sarah woke up early to watch woodhicks move logs through the splash dam. Matthew and Mr. Stephens were joining the drive too. Matthew stood on the creek bank next to her, watching the movement of the lumber. She looked at Matthew. "Have you ever been on a spring drive before?"

Matthew was watching the woodhicks work. "No. It's the first time my father has done this. He wanted to earn extra money to purchase cattle this summer." He bent down to scoop up rocks from the creek bank to save for skipping while they were on the ark.

A large gate was opened in the splash dam. For hours, water and logs rolled down the ramp into the creek below the dam. When the last of the lumber was through the gate, the sun was rising above the eastern mountain. A number of woodhicks pushed the arks into the shallow waters of the creek then waited for the horses and the crew to board. Sarah's father helped her and Matthew onto the last ark. With long pieces of wood, the woodhicks pushed the arks away from the creek banks until the arks floated freely in deeper water. Sarah and Matthew sat on the small porch of their ark to watch the activity.

The sky was blue. The ark floated smoothly through the meandering path between the steep mountains. As the sun rose higher in the sky, Matthew practiced skipping rocks across the creek while Sarah drew scenes of the journey on her tablet. The longer Matthew watched her draw, the more curious he was. He asked to see some of her other drawings.

At first she was reluctant to share them, but she finally put her pencil down and handed him her tablet. He paused on the page where she had drawn a picture of her mother smiling. "She's beautiful, Sarah. Who is this?"

"My mother."

Matthew didn't know anything about Sarah's mother. "Did she die when you were little?"

Sarah looked at the water. She knew it would be natural to make such an assumption. Why else would she and her father be in Slate Run without her mother? "No, my mother—left us last July—one week before my birthday."

Matthew was surprised. "I'm sorry, Sarah. I didn't know."

Sarah looked at the picture she had drawn. "Sometimes I'm angry with her for leaving, but most of the time I'm sad. I wish she were here with father and me."

Matthew turned the page of the tablet. "Sarah, what's the story with this one?" He was looking down at the drawing of a horse running on what appeared to be a cloud. There were wings on each hoof and on his broad back.

She took the tablet from him, her face turning red. "It's embarrassing."

"It's just me, Sarah. I promise I might not laugh."

Her eyes grew big as he emphasized the words *might not laugh,* "Matthew!"

She sat with her back against the ark, her arms crossed.

Matthew seemed genuinely interested. "Please, I won't tell anyone else."

She uncrossed her arms. She took his hands in both of hers. "Swear to me you will never tell anyone."

With all seriousness and a bit of a smirk on his face, he agreed.

Sarah pointed to the top of a mountain. "If you look at the top of the mountain over there, do you see the treetops moving in the breeze?"

Matthew squinted into the sun. He nodded. "Yes."

She continued. "Watch as the breeze comes down the mountain, you can see the path it takes by the movement through the treetops. When it nears us you will be able to hear the sound of the wind in the trees before it hits the valley floor and rushes past us."

She raised their arms as the breeze passed them by. "When I was little, I would sit by the Susquehanna River watching the breeze work through the trees. I would pretend that a wind stallion was running through the forest. When the breeze reached me, I would stretch out my arms and pretend I was riding on the back of the stallion."

She opened her eyes to look over at Matthew to find he was grinning at her. "Pretty silly isn't it? It was my little girl dream I guess."

Matthew released his hands from hers. He took a rock and skipped it across the water. "It's not silly—or crazy—Sarah."

"Then how come you have that silly grin on your face?"

He was looking at the mountain, his expression more serious. "Because I'm always surprised by you Sarah."

Sarah was still getting used to his humor. "Is that a good thing?"

He threw another rock, which skipped six times before hitting the shoreline. "Definitely."

She picked up her tablet of paper again to sketch the lumber floating in the creek. She saw Matthew take a knife and a thick piece of wood from his satchel. He began to whittle something.

Later when the sun was barely visible above the mountain the ark rounded a sharp bend in the gorge where the logs became tightly lodged in the narrow path of the creek. The water level behind the logs rose against the temporary dam. Woodhicks rushed to work at the jam before it became too difficult to loosen. They took narrow sticks with them as they climbed to the top of the lumber to work at loosening logs one at a time. Finally the key log came loose, breaking free a number of logs all at once. Woodhicks scrambled from the pile or jumped into the cold creek as logs blew outward from the pressure of the water that had built up against the lumber. Mr. Stephens was among several men who barely escaped the explosion of lumber in time. It was decided that the arks would pull over for the night.

Progress was slow to Williamsport as they waited several times a day for jams to be cleared. In shallow water, logs became stranded. If the logs were not pushed back into the stream quickly enough, more logs would catch against them, becoming entangled. At dusk the arks docked along the creek banks. They camped five nights. In the morning the arks would catch up to the first logjam and push the lumber downstream.

When the crew reached the town of Jersey Shore, the swift brown waters of Pine Creek merged with the green waters of the Susquehanna River. The pace of the drive quickened on the wide river. When the scenery became familiar to Sarah she put her drawing tablet away. Sarah had forgotten how much she loved living along the banks of the Susquehanna River. She was excited about surprising her cousin Kassie. She tried to describe the sawmills, factories, and farms to Matthew but soon stopped to let him enjoy the scenery. For Matthew, all of the sites were new. He had come to Slate Run from the north in New York State. As the arks floated closer to Williamsport, farmers would stop their fieldwork to wave at the passing crew. Sometimes children would run along the banks, following their path as far as they could.

Sarah was overwhelmed with emotion when the arks came around a bend and in view of Revival Bible Church. She watched her father who was operating the rudder of the ark to see what his reaction might be, but he seemed focused on his task.

Seeing the familiar sites of Williamsport made it seem like everything had just happened. When they passed the Exchange Hotel, Sarah watched the riverbanks closely for Kassie in case she came to see the procession float into town. Sarah knew it was unlikely because Kassie would have no idea they were on the spring drive.

As they neared the main log boom at the other end of town, Sarah could see that the logs were backed up for miles. The arks pulled onto the west shore of the river where they would be disassembled so the lumber from the arks could also be sold to the mills. Sarah's father helped Matthew and her onto the shoreline. "Head to your uncle and aunt's place, Sarah."

"How long will you be, father?"

"Most of the day. I am going to assist in disassembling the arks before I finish for the day."

She stood on the bank to watch the ark leave. She couldn't wait to surprise her cousin and the rest of the family.

Kassie screamed, startling everyone at the lunch table. Five-year-old Elijah jumped in his seat dropping his glass of milk on the table, its contents spilling quickly toward the cloth napkin next to his mother's plate.

Aunt Katherine was about to exert a reprimand when she too saw Sarah standing at the kitchen screen door with Matthew. "Sarah!"

She stood up. Kassie was already opening the door, almost pushing Sarah over with a big hug. "Where did you come from?"

Sarah hugged her cousin tight. Aunt Katherine came over to hug the two of them. "Welcome home, Sarah. We missed you so much!"

Aunt Katherine noticed Matthew standing in the background waiting patiently as the girls shrieked and hugged. "Who is this young man?"

Sarah composed herself. She had forgotten about Matthew. "Sorry, Aunt Katherine, please excuses my manners. This is Matthew Stephens, son of Wilson and Esther Stephens, from Slate Run. He and his father were on the spring drive with us."

"You were on the spring drive? I heard the commotion on the river but would not have guessed that your father and you would be on the drive."

Sarah knew her aunt would not have approved of her brother-in-law's decision to bring a young girl on such a venture. She could see her aunt rehearsing a speech to unleash on her father as soon as he arrived.

"So I'm guessing your father is at the mill helping dismantle the arks?"

"Yes."

"Come inside. We are finishing lunch. I have hot molasses cookies and milk for dessert."

Sarah knew they would be leaving on the train for Slate Run the day after tomorrow, so she spent every moment she could with Kassie, catching up on everything that had happened since she had left Williamsport. Matthew and his father stayed at a boarding house in town. Aunt Katherine insisted that Matthew and his father have meals with the family.

For Elijah, having Matthew there was like having a brother. He continually asked him to throw a ball in the backyard or explore with him in the garden. Matthew discovered quickly Elijah loved all kinds of bugs. They spent hours finding new specimens.

Sarah's father slept in the downstairs parlor. She stayed in Kassie's room, which meant the two girls slept little. Because they were only staying two days, Sarah and her father didn't bother opening the old house. They weren't ready to step into their home just yet. Two days was too short of a time to catch up. Kassie's window overlooked the flower gardens next door. Sarah sat in Kassie's windowsill in the evening while they talked. She remembered how her mother had loved pruning the roses and planting flowers in the garden. Sarah had always thought they had the most beautiful flowers on millionaire row. Although her aunt had done her best to care for it, the garden did not look the same as when her mother had been there. Being near home again made Sarah miss her mother with renewed awareness.

On her last day in town Sarah walked along the riverbanks with Kassie, watching the activity of the woodhicks sorting logs for the sawmills. Her father was at his lumber office by the mills. He returned home midday so he could invite the girls to go to the post office with him. He offered to stop at the general store for penny candy.

They stopped for candy at the general store first, visiting briefly with Mrs. Pratt, who wanted to know all about life in the wilderness. At the post office Kassie and Sarah sat on a bench inside the lobby while John stood in line at one of the mail windows.

A man in front of John was speaking with the clerk. "Do you have a forwarding address for Dave Claythorn?"

Sarah's eyes darted away from Kassie, who was telling her something about school, to the gentleman speaking with the clerk. The balding gentleman wore an expensive three-piece suit and spoke with an unusual accent. "I desperately need to contact him. Do you know of anyone who can help me?"

Sarah heard her father clear his throat. "Sir, I might be able to help you."

The man turned to John. "Thank you, sir—please."

Her father motioned for them to speak outside in private. The gentleman nodded,

"Of course," and quickly followed him outside.

Sarah wanted to follow and listen but knew it would be impolite. Kassie waved a hand in front of Sarah's face. "Sarah, are you paying attention at all?"

Sarah looked back at her frustrated cousin. "Sorry, Kassie. I was distracted by the gentleman my father is talking with outside. Have you ever seen him before?"

Kassie quickly forgave her best friend for the sake of a new drama. She turned in the bench to look out the window. "I've never seen him before."

Sarah pushed her cousin. "You're closest to the door; see if you can hear anything."

They were leaning as close to the door as they could without being seen. Kassie was able to peak around the corner of the doorframe as long as no one was coming. Sarah watched anxiously hoping for some kind of clue. After only a few minutes the man handed a piece of paper to her father, shook hands with him, and walked away.

Kassie turned in her seat to face Sarah. "I could be wrong, but his accent sounded a lot like a teacher from Boston we had a few years back."

Sarah remembered the teacher. "Mr. Pratchett was from Boston! I think you are right!"

Sarah was really puzzled why someone from Boston would be looking for Reverend Claythorn and what information had been given to her father.

The question was still on her mind the next morning when they hugged their family goodbye once again. Sarah reassured Kassie they would be together again. The train whistle blew and Sarah, her father, Mr. Stephens, and Matthew boarded the train for Slate Run.

John was quiet on the train ride to Slate Run. He was aware Sarah and Kassie had noticed the conversation that took place between him and the gentleman from Boston. Sarah hadn't asked him any questions. He reached into his jacket pocket making sure the paper the man from Boston had given him was still there. He knew that when they reached Slate Run he was going to have to confront Reverend Claythorn.

CHAPTER 25

Flood

Sarah and John arrived in Slate Run on May 29 just as a severe storm arrived in the valley. Few people were at the train station in the pouring rain. Uncle Harold was waiting under the overhang at the station to take Sarah, her father, Mr. Stephens, and Matthew to the hotel where their horses were boarding in the barn behind the hotel. They disembarked from the train and rushed over to where he waited. The rain and roaring wind made conversation impossible.

By the time they reached the hotel, their shoes and clothing were soaked. Mr. Stephens and Matthew quickly retrieved their horses and donned rain slicks that Uncle Harold loaned them. Before heading out of the barn, Matthew gently pulled the reigns back on his horse. He looked back at Sarah who was saddling up Duke. He smiled as he spoke, "It seems that whenever we are together, adventure is not too far away. See you, Sarah."

Sarah's face reddened. "Ride safely home, Matthew." She opened the barn door a little wider for him to ride through. Mr. Stephens was right behind him on another horse. She watched until they disappeared into the rain and was surprised at how sad she felt about Matthew leaving.

Sarah and her father left right after the Stephens. They rode on Duke together. The thunder cracked several times overhead, making her jump every time. When they arrived home her father let her down from the saddle before he took Duke to the barn. Glad they had remembered to stack wood inside before they left, Sarah quickly started a fire.

All through the night the thunder boomed between the mountains, rattling their small cabin. Sarah shook under her covers, burying her head in her pillow to block out the flashing lightning and roaring thunder. The single window over her bed lit with the constant flashing of lightning that reached across the sky from cloud to cloud. Sarah slept little. For two days the storms raged over the valley. The wind beat the rain against the side of the house and the tin roof. On the morning of June 1, she checked on Duke and the chicks, and then put on a rain slick so she could inspect the water level in Pine Creek.

When she told her father her plans, he decided to go with her. "I'll walk over with you; I'm curious how the splash dam is holding up."

The town was quiet with most of the woodhicks having gone back to their homes to farm for the summer until the hemlock bark harvest in the winter months. No one was responsible for watching the splash dam. Fast moving water pushed through the open gate in the dam with excess flow building high against the top of the dam and pushing over the edge. Small branches littered the water from islands upstream that had been washed over.

Her father seemed troubled, "That dam won't hold if we get more rain, especially if debris blocks the open gate." She wondered about the other dams north of this one too.

They headed back home. After lunch her father put on his rain slick again. "I have some business to take care of at the office."

He wasn't gone long before Sarah grew restless and decided to ride Duke to the splash dam again. She pushed against the driving curtains of rain to the bridge where she could see things had gotten much worse.

Water was flowing so thick over the top of the dam the structure was buried under the rushing waters. The wagon bridge that ran across the creek was covered in a thin layer of water. The rush of the water and the driving rain was so loud no other sound could be heard above it. She was startled when Duke bumped into Uncle Harold.

"Sarah!" He yelled up to her, surprised to see her alone by the creek. "The dam isn't holding!" He took Duke's reigns to turn the horse around and slapped Duke on the rear. "Go! Now!"

Sarah clung to Duke as he ran home. When she reached the house she jumped down, her heart pounding. She ran through the house, then to the barn.

"Father, father, are you here?"

She threw open the barn doors to let the rooster and the hen run free. She scooped the chicks into a basket. Duke was stomping and whimpering outside as if to hurry her. She hopped onto Duke as a loud explosion came from the direction of the dam. She rode toward the mountain at full speed, the basket of chicks looped around her arm.

God, keep Father safe!

Before Duke reached the edge of the forest, she looked behind her. A wall of water and debris higher than the homes was tearing through the gorge. The last thing she remembered was the scream of Duke as she was ripped off his back, the basket of chicks torn from her grasp.

When John left the house after lunch, he planned on confronting Reverend Claythorn. Reaching into his pocket again to make sure the letter was still there, he mentally rehearsed what he would say. When he stood at Reverend Claythorn's front door, the memories replayed themselves in his head. It had been a year ago that he had stepped onto Reverend Claythorn's porch in Williamsport to go over some church business. He had glanced in a window when no one came to the door. That was when he saw his wife in the reverend's arms, the reverend kissing her. The emotions from that moment rushed through him, making him sick, filling him with hate toward the man. He slammed his fists into a loud knock on the door. He was determined to do what he should have done a year ago.

Reverend Claythorn came to the door quickly; he was visibly shaken to see John standing on the porch. "John—" Before the sentence was finished, John's fist impacted the reverend's chin with enough force to slam the reverend against a small table in the front hallway, which toppled under his weight.

Shocked, Reverend Claythorn quickly scrambled to his feet. "How dare you come into my home and—" He wiped at blood dripping from the corner of his mouth.

He flinched backwards when John reached forward to grab him by the collar. "I should have done that a long time ago, Claythorn."

"Get your hands off of me." Reverend Claythorn pushed John away from him, and then straightened his button up vest. "How dare you assault me in my home, John."

John was not finished yet. "Do you need to be punched again?"

Reverend Claythorn held up a hand to stop John.

John kept his fist to his side. "I'm sparing you what you really deserve."

"I'm well aware of that, John. Will it satisfy you that I'm really sorry for what happened?" Reverend Claythorn nervously entered the parlor where he sat in a chair.

John stood in the doorway with no intention of following, his coat dripping puddles of water onto the polished wood floor.

Reverend Claythorn invited John inside. "Come in, let's talk like civilized men."

John spoke from where he stood. "How can you act so civilized?"

Reverend Claythorn came into the entry hall again but kept a safe distance from John. "John, I don't know how to make amends—."

John looked at the reverend from under the rim of his dripping hat. "It's time for you to leave, Claythorn."

Reverend Claythorn appeared tired. "I didn't know you were in Slate Run—or I would not have come."

John was quietly fuming.

Reverend Claythorn spoke up in the awkward silence. "John, what are you doing in Slate Run? Shouldn't you be looking for your wife? Do you even know where she is?"

Angered at his audacity, John hit the reverend in the jaw.

Reverened Claythorn massaged his jaw. "I don't want to fight you, John—"

John lunged for the reverend. The force of him pushing into Reverend Claythorn landed them both on the kitchen table. Reverend Claythorn pushed his fists against John's chest, but John held him down firmly. He looked down at the reverend waiting, daring him to fight.

Reverend Claythorn raised a fist to his jaw. John continued holding him firmly down. Then the reverend broke loose throwing one fist after the other into John's chest and jaw. Still unable to budge John, the reverend managed to use the full force of his leg against John's chest to push him away. John stumbled backwards from the table. Undaunted, John came after him again as the reverend ran onto the front porch to escape his attacker. John tackled him against the porch railing, which snapped under their weight, sending them both rolling onto the open, muddy ground and into the pouring rain.

A loud roar, greater than the sound of a rushing train came from upstream. They both stopped their fighting to look up. A wall of water higher than the parsonage was crashing down on them. They were only able to run a few steps before the wave fell on the parsonage, breaking it apart, and sweeping them off their feet in a great wall of water. Something large came up under John pushing him to the top of the raging river. He gasped for air, clinging tightly to a large piece of roof. Reverend Claythorn was floating nearby. Without thinking, John reached for the reverend's hand to pull him onto the roof. They both climbed to its peak to straddle it as they rode it downstream. The roof bobbed and dipped dangerously under them, at times almost flipping over. Large pieces of lumber and broken homes rushed past them. A horse helplessly floated by, and John thought he heard a cry from someone in the water.

The water came to a narrow bend in the creek where it built up against the mountain as it tried pushing through. The roof snagged against a log, jerking suddenly to the left. Reverend Claythorn was tossed into the water. He came up gasping for air. This time when John reached out to grab him he was thrown into the water himself. The current that snagged the roof was pulling them toward the shore. With one hand on the reverend, he reached with the other toward a tree leaning out over the water. He used the tree to pull them to shore. Just as they reached shore, the snagged roof came loose and floated past them in pieces. He dragged the reverend safely above the water level then dropped down onto the ground, exhausted.

Sarah was shivering when she woke up, tangled in a clump of branches on the creek bank. Her legs from the knees down were still in the water. Her boots were gone, her calico dress torn and caked with mud. As she started to twist her way out of the branches that held her legs under water, she moaned from pain. Her exposed arms were scratched and bruised. A large, red spot near her thigh soaked through her dress. When she pulled herself free, she lifted her dress high enough to see a large gash on her right thigh. Caked mud on her skin had stopping the bleeding. It was difficult to see how serious the injury was. When she tried to stand, the pain in her leg was strong enough to make her wince, but she was able to put a little weight on it. Sarah cleaned the wound with the hem of her dress then wrapped more cloth around her leg to keep it from bleeding.

She looked along the banks of the rushing water desperately trying to figure out where she was. Nothing familiar was in sight; everything was covered with water. The creek still flowed high and swift, filled with brown debris. Parts of homes were flowing by and Sarah watched in horror as livestock and bodies floated by, struggling for life.

From an island midstream, she heard someone calling out. She could see a man in a tree, holding up the head of a cow above water. The cow was bleating in desperation. There was nothing she could do to help them. She couldn't even call out and be heard above the sound of the water. She felt guilty leaving them, but had to keep moving to find shelter before dark.

Sarah hadn't gone far when she recognized a small voice calling out to her.

"Sarah!"

It was Mason. She wasn't sure where he was, so she stood still listening. When it was quiet she called out. "Mason! Where are you?"

The woods were quickly becoming dark. Mason's call came to her from nearby. "Here! Sarah, here!"

The sound came from behind a large rock. Unable to run, she limped as quickly as she could. Mason was leaning against the side of the rock crying. He was covered in mud. A large gash ran along his right check. Sarah sat down next to him to cradle him in her lap. He cried harder and clung to her dress.

"Moth—er"

He choked through his cries calling out "mother."

Sarah held him closer trying to soothe him by rocking him back and forth. His muddy hand wiped at his tears. He looked up at Sarah.

"Mother and sis were swept away—I —I—couldn't hold on, they were—p—p—pulled away!"

She clung to Mason praying quietly, "Please God, let them be found alive."

She opened her eyes when she heard a familiar neigh. Duke was a few yards away, walking toward them. She put Mason down to call out to him. "Duke!"

She couldn't believe he was still alive. He trotted slowly toward Sarah obviously frightened by his experience. She breathed a prayer of thankfulness. She couldn't carry Mason, especially with her injured leg. When she saw a large rock nearby with a flat top, she told Mason to crawl on top of the rock. She guided Duke to stand next to the rock. "Mason, grab onto Duke's mane and pull yourself up." It took a couple of tries, but he was able to pull himself up onto Duke's back while she held the horse steady.

Without a saddle to assist in her mounting Duke, she also had to mount him from the top of the rock. Sarah did her best to not put pressure on her leg but the movement of mounting Duke opened the wound again. She could feel warm blood oozing into the cloths she had wrapped around the wound.

Once on Duke she paused to look around. She was relieved at the sight of smoke from the mountaintop; they were down slope from the Stephens' ranch. Mason was already slumped over in front of her, exhausted.

Before they had gone even halfway up the mountain, they spotted Matthew on his horse.

"Matthew, over here!" Sarah was relieved to see another familiar face.

Matthew quickly turned his horse in their direction. He came alongside them, slipping a rope around Duke's neck so he could lead them home. When they reached the Stephens' ranch, Matthew's mother came outside to meet them, quickly taking Mason from Sarah.

Matthew helped Sarah down from Duke, linking an arm around her shoulder to help her inside to the fire. He left the house, quickly riding off on his horse again. A number of people were already inside, huddled in blankets near the fire. She saw Mr. Wagner, Mr. Milton, and a number of men from the Pennsylvania Joint Land Company, but her father was not among them; neither were her aunt, uncle, or Janine. She was filled with worry as Mrs. Stephens handed her a hot tin of tea. She sipped the hot liquid, wrapping her fingers around the tin to soak in its warmth.

Mrs. Stephens must have seen Sarah's concern. "Sarah, I don't know if Matthew told you, but before he found you, he came across your father on the mountain looking for you. He headed back out to let him know you are here."

Sarah felt relieved. She was still worried about her other family members. "It's hard to believe anyone survived the terrible wave that came down on the town. I still have an aunt and uncle and little niece out there." Mrs. Stephens tried to assure her that people were still finding their way to the ranch.

It was long after dark when the door opened and her father rushed inside. She looked up from her place near the fire. "Father!"

He hugged her tight. "Sarah, I can't bear the thought of ever losing you."

Sarah reached her arms around her Father's neck. She felt the same. "I love you too, father."

It was with surprise she looked past her father into the eyes of Reverend Claythorn. When the reverend noticed her glance, he left the house.

Leia

"*Mother*" *by Sarah Richardson*

CHAPTER 26

The Way Home

Caroline and Leia were urged to leave a day early by the stagecoach master. They had come to the general store to see if there was any news on the water levels up north. Mrs. Rose, the general store owners' wife, was measuring flour into a cotton bag when she saw the stagecoach master come inside from the rain.

"Ladies, just a minute, I think he can help you."

She was still scooping flour when she yelled loudly across the store. "George!"

George was a tall man covered in a layered leather rain slick, hat, and boots. The only part of him visible was his ruddy tan face and full grey beard. Although the women jumped at Mrs. Rose's holler, he responded unfazed, coming directly to the counter.

"George, these ladies have tickets for the stage tomorrow but are concerned about the water levels in the creek."

He turned to the ladies, removing his hat at the same time. "Ladies, I'm George Manning, the stage master. I'm afraid that I will not be able to go north tomorrow."

He could see the immediate alarm in Leia's eyes.

"I apologize but the water levels in the creek are already dangerously high and the rain is still coming down. I am hoping I make it out safely today."

Leia's mind was racing with a plan.

"Mr. Manning is there any way we could take the stage today? We can be ready within the hour. It is of utmost importance I reach Williamsport." Leia's voice quivered a bit, but her determination kept her from too much emotion.

Mr. Manning looked at the women. He heard the desperation in Leia's request. "I'll tell you what. I have only one rider today and the postal delivery for Williamsport. I'll order a hot breakfast at the boarding house. That will give you two hours."

Leia smiled. "Thank you, Mr. Manning. We will be ready."

He turned to leave. "I won't wait any longer than two hours."

It wasn't until she was settled into the stagecoach with her mother, a gentleman from the mill, and Nevi in a closed basket under the seat, that she started to worry about her arrival in Williamsport.

"Mother, what if—" Leia's eyes darted toward the gentleman across from them who settled into his seat, pulling his hat over his eyes to rest. She lowered her voice.

"—What if it doesn't work out?"

Her mother remained a calming companion, holding Leia's hand in her own. "I can't tell you, Leia, that everything will work out the way we want it too, but I am confident that God is in control of this situation. Worrying about the unknown won't make anything better."

Leia was amazed at her mother's composure. She knew her mother must have her own anxiety at the prospect of meeting family members she had never met before. "I know, Mother, but it is so difficult to not worry. I miss John and Sarah so much." She took the opportunity to bring up another subject on her mind. "Mother I haven't known how to tell you this, but the day father was killed and I ran away—" Leia looked out the window at the swollen Lycoming Creek. The rain was continuing down in heavy sheets. They were crossing a bridge that sat only a foot above the raging waters. "I told you about being taken in by Lillian and Graham Dalton. What I did not tell you is, when they found me, I told them my name was Mary. My family doesn't know anything about my childhood before the Daltons. Leia is a person none of them know."

Her mother looked at her with shock. "Not even John?"

"No, I blocked out my memories of the past. I didn't want to remember how father beat us. I was afraid that if I told the truth about my past, I would have to remember everything."

"Leia—" her mother paused. "Your family should know your real story." Before she could continue the stagecoach came to an abrupt stop, almost throwing them out of their seats. The gentleman sleeping across from them woke abruptly from his sleep. Leia lifted the window flap to look outside. Mr. Manning was stepping down from his high seat in the front of the stagecoach. The gentleman decided to see what was going on. Leia could see they were at the edge of a bridge across from a small settlement. Water was rushing over the bridge in a thin muddy sheet. Mr. Manning and the gentleman were studying the bridge, debating if it was safe to cross. Leia could hear parts of the conversation through the wind and the rain.

Mr. Manning was concerned about the safety of his passengers but also the fact that if they became stranded on this side of the bridge, they would have nowhere to go. They would be trapped for days. Mr. Manning decided they would quickly cross before conditions worsened. The gentleman boarded the stagecoach again. Mr. Manning whipped the reigns against the four horses. He knew the urgency with which they needed to cross. Everyone was silent as the stagecoach splashed through the water flowing over the bridge. Debris was pilling against the small railing on the bridge, water building higher against it. Leia pointed up stream to a large object in the water coming toward them fast. Mr. Manning saw it too. He cracked the reigns again, yelling out to the horses, "Yaw!"

When it came closer they could make out the broken parts of a house rushing toward the bridge. Leia reached under the seat for Nevi's basket and held tightly to her mother's hand. The horses were protesting at the danger, racing toward land. People from the village were standing nearby watching the stagecoach cross.

Leia felt the whole bridge shake when the house hit. The stagecoach crossed over to land barely in time. With a great moan the bridge gave way behind them, disappearing under the rushing waters. Mr. Manning could see another wave, higher than the last one, coming downstream. He pushed the horses harder. A stagecoach wheel became lodged in mud making it impossible to go further. He yelled to the passengers, "Everyone out!" Townspeople were already at the stagecoach to help. Mr. Manning released the horses from their harness.

Leia gave someone the basket with Nevi then turned for her mother. The stagecoach suddenly tilted at a steep angle when the wheel of the stagecoach sunk further into the mud. Caroline slid deeper into the compartment away from the door. Leia grabbed her mother's hand to pull her out. A wave of water came over the roof of the stagecoach tearing Caroline from Leia's grasp and pushing the stagecoach into the raging flood. It rolled upside down in the water. Leia stood on the shoreline searching the waters. Her mother's head come up from the water behind the stagecoach. "Mother!" she jumped into the torrent after her mother who was being carried downstream.

CHAPTER 27

Recovery

At the entrance of the ranch was an iron archway topped with the words *Stephens Ranch*. A wood split rail fence bordered the forty-acre property. A dirt road wound through a grassy meadow that sloped uphill to the ranch house and barn. The ranch was busy with activity as people found their way to the only safe place from the flooded valley. Limping horses, cows, dogs, and even someone carrying a pig, came to the ranch. John and Reverend Claythorn helped by caring for the animals coming in with the people.

Sarah helped Mrs. Stephens feed everyone. Sarah took soup out to the barn for new arrivals. As she walked from the house to the barn, Mason held onto the back of her skirt keeping his eyes on the dirt road, waiting for his family to appear. Mason bumped into Sarah when she stopped at the barn door to open the latch.

Inside the barn, blankets lined the floor. It was quiet inside, most everyone in shock or sleeping on the floor. Some hay from the loft fluttered to the floor, and Sarah saw a bare foot push over the edge. It seemed the whole town of Slate Run was here. Sarah carried a platter of soup bowls, lowering it to anyone who was awake. Her injured leg kept her from squatting down, but she bent forward with her back as much as possible. When she emptied the tray, she returned to the house for more.

Sarah noticed how tired Mrs. Stephens looked. She had been making soup and wrapping wounds for hours. "Mrs. Stephens, I can do more than distribute food. Why don't you rest while I finish the stew you started?"

Mrs. Stephens didn't even hesitate. "Thank you, Sarah. I am not sure how much longer I can keep going."

Mrs. Stephens sat in a chair at the breakfast table and put her head down for only a moment. The front door opened. Matthew was helping a young man through the door. Sarah looked up anxiously but didn't recognize the man who cradled an injured arm. Sarah continued to stir the stew as Mrs. Stephens helped the man to a place by the fire where she could look at his arm. Dusk came. She helped serve a dinner of beans and biscuits. Late in the evening Sarah found a place near the kitchen to rest. She snuggled Mason by her side hoping he would sleep. Thankfully he did.

Sarah rested with her eyes closed but couldn't fall asleep. The front door opened letting a rush of cool air come in. Sarah squinted her eyes open to see her father and Reverend Claythorn come in. She watched them sit quietly at the kitchen table holding hot tins of tea in their hands. Reverend Claythorn looked up from his cup at John.

"Why did you rescue me from the water? If you had let me go, no one would have known any different. I would be out of your life for good."

Sarah's back was to the table. She opened her eyes and stared at the fireplace. She was picturing her father's face as he sat holding his hot drink.

Her father answered Reverend Claythorn. "I don't know why I reached a hand out to you, Claythorn. I really don't like you."

Reverend Claythorn responded quickly. "John, from now on, call me Dave. It doesn't feel appropriate for you to continue calling me Reverend Claythorn or even Claythorn. You saved my life."

Her father answered again. "Just because I saved you doesn't mean that things are fine between us. I'm not ready to address you as Dave yet."

Her father was silent for a moment before he answered the reverend. "To answer your question of why I saved you, before you arrived in Slate Run, there was a fire at the boarding house. My brother-in-law risked his life to save the drunk that caused the fire. When he was asked why he saved the man's life at risk to his own, he said simply, 'it was the right thing to do'."

Reverend Claythorn sounded surprised. "The right thing to do?"

Her father continued. "I have thought about the incident at the boarding house since it happened, wondering if I would do the same thing if I was in my brother-in-law's place. It seems to me if you have the opportunity to save someone it shouldn't matter who they are."

It was quiet again. Sarah imagined they were drinking their tea as they were thinking about what had been said.

"John, I owe you an apology. But an apology isn't enough for what has happened. I have been a very prideful, sinful man. I didn't think about the effect my actions would have on so many people."

Sarah listened intently for her father's response. He instead brought up the incident at the post office during their last visit to town. "I met a gentleman at the post office in Williamsport during the spring drive." He paused. Sarah looked in the direction of the table. Her father was pulling a soggy paper from his shirt pocket. "Mr. Brian Davis from Boston gave me a letter for you."

Reverend Claythorn was visibly surprised at the mention of Mr. Brian Davis. "Did he say what he wanted?"

John handed the fragile letter to Reverend Claythorn who slowly took it from him. "He wanted to know where you had gone. He asked that I give this letter to you."

Reverend Claythorn opened the letter carefully so it wouldn't tear along the wet folds. He was quiet as he read the letter. When he finished reading it he left the table. Sarah watched him walk out the front door. She couldn't sleep, wondering what the letter had said.

The letter from Boston changed Reverend Claythorn. After dinner the next day, he approached John, "Can we talk outside?"

It was dusk, the air outside cool. John followed reverend Claythorn through the field behind the ranch. Peepers called from a woodsy swamp nearby. "You and your family have unfortunately been affected by my actions. It is time I take responsibility for things." He paused. "Thank you for delivering the letter. Because of it I have made some decisions, one of which is to leave my job as a minister." Reverend Claythorn brushed his hand across the tops of the high meadow grass, the evening dew collecting on his skin. "There is a story behind the letter you gave me."

John remained quiet.

Reverend Claythorn began. "I grew up in a privileged home in Boston. My father was a lawyer and held a position in the city government for years. My family was well known. Our estate rivaled the governor's palace. My father graduated from Harvard with Samuel Green who was later elected mayor of Boston. He used his friendship with Mr. Green to get me a position under the governor. But I was uninterested in government—a fact my father chose to ignore."

John looked at Reverend Claythorn, "That must have been difficult for you. Did you know what you wanted to do?"

Reverend Claythorn was surprised John would express interest in his story. "While at Harvard I came across the writings of Dwight L. Moody, from Northfield, Massachusetts. I couldn't get enough of his writings. It was from those readings I knew I wanted to be a preacher." He watched fireflies begin to fill the darkening sky. "When I shared this with my father he told me it was foolish for a privileged man like myself to throw away the connections and opportunities I was born with for a profession any average person could do."

John interrupted. "Then how did you end up in the ministry?"

"While at Harvard, I took every Bible class they offered. It was there I met a young lady, Lorraine Davis, who had grown up an orphan but was taken in by one of the upper-class families in Boston. When I introduced her to my family and made known my intention to marry her, my parents were upset. I will never forget the words my father yelled to me later that evening,

'She might live in privilege but she was born in lower-class society. That is part of a person's heritage that never goes away. She might seem fine, but at some point it will become apparent.'

I argued with him to no avail. He claimed it was questionable how a woman with her background came to live with such a privileged family. He thought she was interested in me for money. I could not reason with him."

John asked Reverend Claythorn about Lorraine's last name. "Is she related to the Brian Davis who wrote the letter?"

"Yes."

Reverend Claythorn stood quietly in the grass. He knew it was time to be truthful about his past. "I continued to see Lorraine in secret. When she became pregnant, both my parents and hers rejected me. The pregnancy was proof to my father she was still lower class. Lorraine was taken away to an undisclosed location until the baby was born. When born, the baby was given away. My father said he would never talk to me again.

It was then I left Boston and travelled to Kansas to be a missionary to the Indians. I knew no one in Kansas would care who I was or which part of society I was from."

Reverend Claythorn swallowed hard as the emotions built up inside. "My mother sent me a letter while I was in Kansas to tell me of my father's passing. She wanted me to come home. I started to come home but stopped when I reached Williamsport. I wasn't ready to go back to Boston. When I saw all the activity around the lumberyards in town and how hard the people worked, I thought I found a place I could be happy. The anger I had against my father was strong. Everything I did was to prove him wrong. I wanted to control my life. Mary reminded me of Lorraine—"

Dave looked at John wondering if John would hit him again. He even wondered if he shouldn't have said Mary's name. "The man you met at the post office, Mr. Brian Davis, is Lorraine's father. The letter explained that Lorraine died from influenza last year."

Reverend Claythorn paused again, looking at the stars overhead.

"Her son was never given up for adoption. He lives with Mr. and Mrs. Davis in their home in Boston. Mr. Davis hopes I will come home to my son whom Lorraine named Dave. He says he forgives me." Reverend Claythorn looked at John. "I find myself the undeserving recipient of abundant grace. If you hadn't saved me from the water, I would not be able to return home to my son."

Reverend Claythorn hoped John would be able to forgive him someday. They parted ways, Reverend Claythorn retiring to the barn, and John sitting at the kitchen table inside, for most of the night.

CHAPTER 28

Living Again

Mr. Stephens and Matthew found Uncle Harold the next morning while they were searching the mountainside for survivors, as they had been every day since the flood. Uncle Harold was alive but unconscious. A bruised knot rose up from his skull running from temple to cheekbone on his left side. Matthew helped lift him onto the saddle of one of the horses to bring him up the mountain to the ranch house. Mason was headed out to the barn with Sarah when they saw them coming.

"Father!" He ran to the horse carrying his Uncle Harold. Mason was scared at the sight of his unconscious father, "Is he dead?"

Mr. Stephens comforted him quickly. "Mason, he's alive. He's just sleeping."

Reverend Claythorn helped lift Uncle Harold down from the saddle. Sarah held onto Mason to give the men room as they carried her uncle into the house. Mrs. Stephens checked the wound on his head. When she was done, Mason curled up next to his father and slept. Sarah checked on him throughout the day as she helped cook meals again. There was still no sign of Aunt Virginia or Janine.

Near dusk she went with her father to an overlook where they could see Slate Run. The water still ran high and brown in Pine Creek but only a few feet over its natural riverbanks. The valley floor was brown with mud. The church and the post office were the only structures still standing. All of the homes along the river, including their home and barn, were gone.

"Father, do you think the trains will be able to get through?"

John shook his head. "I would assume that most of the railroad bridges were washed out."

Sarah breathed deep. "What are we going to do?"

John reached over to hold his daughters hand. "One step at a time, we are all going to help each other rebuild the town."

They walked back to the house under an orange sunset. Sarah thought about her aunt's theory of finding joy in the common hours. Her aunt would have enjoyed watching this sunset regardless of what had happened.

Uncle Harold woke that evening. Mason was the first to observe his fathers' eyes opening. Sarah saw Mason react. She and her father were at Uncle Harold's side within seconds. He looked somewhat confused at his surroundings, having never been to the Stephens' ranch before. Sarah caught him up with what had happened. She wanted to ask if he knew about Aunt Virginia and Janine. Mrs. Stephens brought some fresh water in a tin for him to slowly sip.

He sat up to take a sip then quickly sunk back down on the blankets. He remembered the flood and why he was here. Sarah took his hand.

He looked at her and her father and Mason.

"After I saw you by the creek I headed toward the hotel. When the water slammed into us, Virginia was running with Janine in her arms with Mason running alongside them. I saw them knocked off their feet by the wave. Seconds later I was also taken into the wave. When I came up from the water, choking the stuff out of my lungs, I was being carried quickly downstream. I could see Mason clinging to a tree branch at the edge of the water just ahead of me. He was holding his mother's hand with all of his might. Virginia still had Janine in her arms. Debris from a barn slammed into the girls taking them under the water. I cried out hoping to see them come back up for air, but they did not—."

Uncle Harold could barely finish. "Something struck me in the head. I don't remember how I came here."

Sarah was holding the tears inside.

Uncle Harold was still in shock. "I know that they are with Baby Joseph now, but—" he became quiet.

Her father reached a hand over to his brother-in-law. He couldn't speak either.

Uncle Harold looked at his son whose tears were falling down his cheeks. He caressed his son's face with his rough hand. "Mason, you are a brave young man. The last act toward your mother and sister was one of courage as you tried to save them."

Mason curled up against his father's flannel shirt crying. Sarah wiped at the tears she could no longer hold back.

CHAPTER 29

New Beginnings

Within a week most of the survivors left the Stephens Ranch for the valley. Sarah was up early on the morning she and her father planned on heading back to town. She walked through meadow to the valley overlook. The morning dew and sun were highlighting spider webs that hung gracefully between sprigs of flowers and stray wheat. She could see Matthew walking through the field toward her. She was glad for his company.

"I'm sorry for your loss, Sarah." He spoke quietly, looking out over the valley.

They were both looking at the destruction below. It was a clear morning, but the valley was still in shadows. She felt the loss of her aunt and cousin so strongly. At times she still held out hope they would be found, but she knew she was having difficulty dealing with the truth of their deaths.

Matthew reached his hand toward Sarah, something in his palm. "I made something for you."

He held a horse of carved wood with wings on its body and hooves, legs bent in a full run.

She was taken by complete surprise. "You made my Wind Stallion!"

Matthew smiled a little, "I started carving this for you while we were on the spring drive. It was too compelling of an idea for me to resist."

Without thinking first, she swept her arms around his neck in a quick embrace. "Thank you, Matthew. I love it!" Embarrassed at what she had just done, she pulled her arms away.

Matthew looked down at his shoes. "Race you back to the house!"

She stood there watching him run through the field. "Not fair, I can't run yet!"

Sarah walked as quickly as she could with her injured leg, holding the wind stallion tightly in her right hand. A hot breakfast was waiting for them inside, after which they said their goodbyes. It was time to help rebuild the town.

The church was cleaned first, to provide housing for people while they rebuilt homes. Four feet of mud had to be shoveled out, swept, and then scrubbed away to provide a shelter. The Stephens sent extra blankets downhill for people to sleep on.

A group of men rode north to Wellsboro to retrieve food and supplies. The provisions could not come quickly enough. Everyone was busy; some were building shelters, some cooking large meals, and others providing medical attention to the sick and injured.

The cemetery on the hill grew by ten. Two stones were laid for Aunt Virginia and Janine although their bodies were never recovered. It took a month for everyone working together, to rebuild the town. When he felt it was the appropriate time, Reverend Claythorn left to reunite with his son in Boston.

Groups of railroad men came through, repairing tracks. They brought with them stories of survival and loss from all along the Pine Creek gorge.

Sarah overheard the story of a woman and a tame bear surviving the flood by climbing high in a tree. When she heard about the devastation in Williamsport, she was worried for her family there.

When the work of rebuilding was finally settling down, Sarah walked to the graveyard to visit the graves of Aunt Virginia and Janine. She walked with her head down looking at her shoes in front of her, one step forward, then another. Somehow through all the pain and loss, she still walked forward.

She stopped near the stacked-rock border of the graveyard. The waist-high walls were overgrown with green moss. Vines blossomed here and there with pink and white wild roses, a sharp contrast to the large area above the creek that had been stripped of life and coated with mud. Through a small gap in the wall she walked into the graveyard. Aunt Virginia and Janine's graves were at the far end. She looked up to see her uncle standing in front of the two stones. She paused, unsure if this was a good time to come. Harold motioned her over when he saw her.

He held a hat in his hands, his fingers mindlessly crimping the edges of the hat. Sometimes he looked up at the sky, his lips moving in silent prayers. Sarah didn't know what to say. She stared at the names on the stones.

Virginia Plumb: September 14, 1854 – June 1, 1889
Janine Plumb: January 10, 1884 – June 1, 1889

Jacob spoke first. "Virginia would not want you to be angry at God because of this."

Sarah remained silent, too emotional to speak. He continued to look at the stones while he spoke. "I keep thinking that Janine is in heaven with perfect eyes, seeing her mother for the first time."

Jacob started to leave but turned one last time and smiled at Sarah,

"If there is a piano in heaven she's probably playing 'Mary Had a Little Lamb' to the angels." With that he left the graveyard.

Sarah sat in front of Aunt Virginia's gravestone for a while then stared up at the now clear sunny skies of early June. A robin swooped in to grab up a worm from the moist soil, after which it cocked its head at her then flew away. The dry warm air brushed against her arms then pushed old leaves along the ground. New spring grass grew thick, sprinkled with yellow dandelions. Sarah remembered Janine clapping her hands when she heard that the little turtle was swimming free in the creek; she could see the joy on Janine's face as she played the piano.

Aunt Virginia had been the mother Sarah didn't have for the past year. All the hours spent in the kitchen listening to her words of wisdom, learning to punch and roll bread or churning fresh butter, were valuable hours she would have never had if her father hadn't moved them to Slate Run. She sat in front of their stones quietly for a long time, remembering.

A train finally arrived in late June with supplies of mail and newspapers from Williamsport. The headlines read:

RUIN IN WILLIAMSORT
Five Million Dollars Loss on Lumber Alone. An Epidemic Feared.

Pictures showed Third Street under water as well as the devastation of the sawmills. A place called Johnstown, in western Pennsylvania, was completely devastated when a dam north of the town broke.

Mr. Milton had a letter for her father when they stopped at the post office; it was from Uncle Jacob. He sat on a log with Sarah next to him, as he read the letter out loud.

Dear John,
News coming from the north is not good. We all fear for
you and Sarah and Harold and Virginia and the children.

Much sleep will be lost until we hear that you are all alive and well.

Although the news from Williamsport is filled with destruction, our homes and lives were spared on 4th Street. The sawmill is gone, fortunately with no loss of any of our workers' lives. I had sent everyone home to be safe with their families before the flood came through. Many lives in the city and surrounding areas were lost and many others are still missing or homeless. Fear of disease is rampant because of the dead livestock that litter the edges of the river and the streets. The boom broke, sending tons of lumber into the streets of the city or downstream. It will be with great effort the lumber is returned to the correct mills. Military help is being sent to assist with rebuilding the city and helping the wounded and homeless. Revival Bible Church is gone without a trace of its foundation.

The following news I share with you is both joyous and difficult. It is too complicated to share the details, in this letter, of how things came about, but Mary is here with us.

Sarah's father paused to look at her. She grabbed his arm.

"Read on father, we have to see what has happened to mother."

I urge you to come home as soon as you are able. We are so happy she is returned to us, but it is with great urgency I share with you how ill she has fallen. She is taken with a fever. We have been unable to learn anything except she was caught in the flood. It is a miracle she was able to survive and we pray she will see future days with her family. Please do not delay to come home.

Your brother,
Jacob

Sarah's father closed the letter. She was still resting on her father's arm. "Father. Can we go home?"

The railroad had prioritized the reconstruction of tracks and bridges in the gorge; because of this, Sarah and her father were able to secure a train ticket for the next morning. Because everything was lost in the flood, there wasn't anything to pack for the journey. Sarah worried about leaving Duke in Slate Run but Uncle Harold assured her that he and Mason would bring Duke to them next month.

The Stephens had been helping with the rebuilding of Slate Run. Mr. Stephens and Matthew were still in town the next morning when it was time for the train to leave. Not knowing if she would ever see Matthew again made the parting difficult. She gave him a drawing of their ranch she had done while they were sheltered there.

He loved it. "It's beautiful Sarah. I will treasure this."

She wanted to go home, but she wasn't ready to say goodbye. "Matthew, I hope we see each other again someday."

Then he smiled his silly grin that reminded her of the day he had laughed at her after she was sprayed by the skunk. "Don't worry, Sarah. We are meant to meet again."

His "wind horse" was safely in a pocket where she could be sure it wouldn't be lost. Matthew left with his father when Uncle Harold and Mason came to say their goodbyes. Mason clung to Sarah. When the train whistle blew Uncle Harold had to pry Mason's arms away from her neck. The rest of the goodbyes were said through the cabin windows of the train. She watched Mason and her uncle standing on the station platform until the train turned a corner and Slate Run disappeared from her sight.

John cleared his throat to get her attention, "I hope you don't mind, Sarah, but I've been keeping something from you."

She turned away from the window to look at a piece of paper her father held in his hands. Her eyes filled with surprise.

"Father, I thought all my drawings had been lost in the flood! How—?"
In his hand was the picture of Mary looking into the distance.

"What about the day I was looking for that picture in the barn? Had you already taken it?"

He looked at the picture he held in his hands. It had somehow survived the flood, folded in a shirt pocket. "I saw it hanging in the barn after your accident with the skunk. There was something about it that brought good memories of Mary."

Sarah couldn't speak.

John made a commitment to his daughter. "In many ways, it won't be easy to go back, but I promise you, Sarah, I'm going to be a better father and a better husband. I will do whatever it takes for us to be a family again."

She reached over to hold his hand then pushed her boots against the back of the seat in front of them. She was brimming over with hope and excitement for the first time in a very long time.

"Sarah, you can't make the train go any faster."

Sarah rested her back against her seat to watch the mountains and the creek go by. She reflected on the past year in Slate Run. She remembered meeting Mason and him hollering out that she was "pretty!" —and Mason belly-down in the dirt above the turtle mound. She could feel the touch of Janine's hand resting lightly on her own while she played the piano for her. She could see the little eyes of the hummingbird she had rescued from the dining room, as it looked up at her before it flew away. Then she thought about all the times in the kitchen with Aunt Virginia, all the hours by the fire with her father in the evenings. It was in those common hours she found joy in life again. She smiled. The train traveled through the curves of the gorge, each curve opening to another fold of mountains as they headed home to Mother.

AFTERWARD

It was in the shadows of the wooded mountains in the Pine Creek gorge *The Common Hours* began to take shape. The first draft was 25 pages long. I was 14 years old.

My family had moved from a big city in Texas to a town in Pennsylvania named Jersey Mills, with 35 permanent residents. I entertained myself during the summer months writing, while sitting in a lawn chair at the edge of Pine Creek. The original story, written from a very young point of view, was about Sarah and her "wind stallion".

As the years passed the story came and went through my mind. I headed to college, met my future husband, moved to Arizona, and adopted three children. Then one day in 2011, the story of Sarah and the wind stallion came back, but it had changed with me.

Writing *The Common Hours* was an enjoyable experience. It was a journey back into my childhood remembering what it was like living in the gorge. I hope you find joy reading it, and I hope you find joy in your every day common hours.

BOOK CLUB STUDY GUIDE

Chapters 1-6:
> Why do you think Mary chose to leave her family?
> Who were Sarah and John blaming for what happened, if anyone?
> What were the feelings John was dealing with when the deacons came for a visit?

Chapters 7-11:
> What is the memory that Leia recalls to her mother?
> How has the way her father treated her affected her adult life?
> What defines your worth?
> How is John's relationship with his daughter after they move?

Chapters 12-16:
> How might hearing Ruby's story help Leia with her own past?
> What was the idea that Aunt Virginia gave Sarah about life?

Chapters 17-21:
> Why do you think Leia is acting somewhat like a child in this chapter?
> How is John dealing with his feelings?
> Reverend Claythorn shows up. Have you ever thought you had gotten over something only to have an event happen that brings it up all over again?

Chapters 22-25:

What was Leia feeling when she went with her mother to church?

What brought about Leia's change? Was this sudden or gradual?

Is John justified in fighting the Reverend?

Is it surprising that John saves Reverend Claythorn from the flood?

Chapters 26-28:

Why is Reverend Claythorn sharing his story? Does it change how you feel about him?

Have you ever felt more compassion when you hear someone's story?

Has John forgiven Reverend Claythorn?

How do you know when you have forgiven someone?

Bonus question: Who was the villain in this book?

WORKS CITED

Lowry, Robert. *Shall We Gather at the River*. 1864.
Tome, Philip. *Pioneer Life or Thirty Years a Hunter*. Stackpole Books, 2006.
Polly Wolly Doodle. Harvard student songbook. 1880.
1 Corinthians 13:4-8, (King James Version).

CPSIA information can be obtained at www.ICGtesting.com
Printed in the USA
LVOW04s1448240615

443698LV00016B/804/P